Richard typed furiously on his holographic keyboard attempting to apply full forward time-thrust on the control. "No response," he shouted, "it's stuck in time!" He quickly checked the other functions. Everything showed normal parameters.

Elise spun in her chair checking each of the readouts on the 360-degree holo display. Richard was right. Everything showed normal operation. She bit her lower lip and tasted blood. Something somewhere had to show what was wrong. Something made the chronometer stop. She looked into Richard's expectant eyes. Now what?

John Meyers

ii

Now What?

A Time Travel
Mystery Adventure

John Meyers

John Meyers

To order additional copies of this book, contact:
Moss Canyon
www.mosscanyon.com

CHAPTER 1

Ten... nine... eight...

The ABBI System's voice called out the numbers in a calming feminine voice... steady and mellow...

Richard Graham wasn't feeling particularly steady and mellow at the moment, though. He fidgeted nervously as he sat, perched up on a swivel chair in his cubicle, headset and touch gloves on, eyes scanning quickly over the floating 360-degree holographic display around him, watching rows of colorful pulsing readouts. He kept one hand poised above a single red holographic computer key; finger pointed at the ready. His touch gloves sensitive to "touching" the holographic display keyboard. His other hand was clenched at his side. Both hands were sweaty.

Seven... six... five...

Wende Merrill sat in her own cubicle, in front of her own holographic display hovering in the air around her. She also wore a headset and touch gloves and her hands danced in the air across the holographic display as she enabled various ghostly buttons and keys.

She concentrated on the receding display numbers following the audio countdown. A wisp of long, dark hair fluttered across her face, but she ignored it. The erratic flickering of numbers and words on the rest of the display held her attention. Her eyes flicking back and forth to watch the readout of the countdown. A bead of perspiration trickled down her back between her shoulder blades.

Four... three...

Across the sterile white room, Doctor Elise McAllister also sat in a cubicle, surrounded by her own shimmering holo display, softly vocalizing commands to ABBI; the difference between her cubicle and the others being that she alone had a virtual window to observe the two-foot elongated metallic capsule that currently sat in the resonance chamber just beyond where she stood. She brushed some long brown hair away from her ears and listened intently to the voice calling off the countdown. Her eyes never left the image on the window display in front of her. She stared almost hypnotically at the sleek lines of the capsule, its gleaming shell...

Two... one... initiate...

Richard eased a finger down on the red holographic key. He felt as if the pressures of the entire project, success or failure, were now solely upon his shoulders. He stared at his floating display; eyes checking the steady green row of lights above him – no alarm yet – then locking on the chronometer willing it to move.

Wende tensed every muscle in her body and was surprised to find that she was holding her breath.

Elise gasped at what she was seeing, not expecting the beauty she saw after years of assembling hardware and programming software. The capsule shimmered, then slowly dissolved in a rainbow of metamorphic colors as its molecules dissipated in a rippling warp of time. The colors undulated in waves, then the capsule was gone.

Elise stared for a moment at the now blank display. With the disappearance of the capsule, ABBI's voice announced, "Time reversal," and the chronometer had slowly begun to register. 2045... 2044... 2043...

"Easy, Richard, easy." Elise's voice sounded calm and cool,

belying the churning cauldron of nerves boiling inside her.

Could it be? Could the years of project design and experimentation finally be paying off? Elise had been working for Doctor Bruce and General Amalgamated Laboratories since her graduation from M.I.T. when she was twenty-seven. That was seven years ago and since then, there had been nothing in her life but work. She enjoyed the attention of several men, including Richard, but only distantly, second to her research. Of all the exciting frontiers being opened – the deepest oceans, limitless space – nothing could match the sheer electric excitement of time travel.

The inexhaustible research possibilities had always held a special fascination for Elise. Exploring the past firsthand to learn from mistakes, tragedies... and the mere thought of travel into the future put her mind into its own time warp. But, along with the fascinations were also the disturbing fears of traveling to the past and making a change in history, however minute, that could alter the course of events. There were two classic paradoxes: the casual loop where a future event is the cause of a past event, which in turn is the cause of a future event. Both events then exist in space-time, but their origin cannot be determined. And the Grandfather Paradox: What if events were affected in such a way that Einstein were never born? Or the Founding Fathers? Or herself?

ABBI's voice quietly called off the receding years. 2043... 2042... 2041... 2040... 2039...

The color was beginning to return to Wende's cheeks as she spoke for the first time since the countdown. "We've done it!" she cried. "We've sent a capsule back into time!"

Richard spoke now, too. "We *have* done it, Elise. Look at the chronometer. 1787, here we come!"

Elise was hesitant to be too optimistic. "Okay, let's not get too excited, yet. Stay focused." Words that she didn't feel.

Wende looked disparagingly at her supervisor. "Elise, surely you don't dispute our success in sending the capsule back in time?"

"I didn't say that we're not successful. I just said let's not get too excited."

"Oh, come now," Richard said, "you can't ignore the fact that the capsule is indeed gone. You witnessed it yourself." His face opened in awe. "What was it like?"

Elise looked at her two technicians. Their faces were aglow like excited children. She had no trouble describing the scene as it was etched indelibly in her mind. "The capsule seemed to turn into liquid satin then turned a myriad of sparkling colors, then just dissolved slowly, rippling like waves of water. Then, it was gone from sight."

"Oh, it must have been marvelous," Wende exclaimed. "We've done it! We'll all be rich and famous! At least famous, won't we?" she laughed.

Elise watched the chronometer a moment before answering.

2020... 2019... 2018... 2017...

"Until we can retrieve the capsule and examine it for traces of dust and date it, we don't know where the capsule is. It could have been immediately destroyed by unknown forces. Maybe it remained intact without any complications. We are going to have to man a flight and observe firsthand, gather evidence, and then we will really have achieved something."

Richard was slightly amused. He had been with the lab for five years, had great hopes for the project, and had watched Elise tear herself apart over the whole thing, agonizing over every detail no matter how elementary or complex. Glancing at Elise, Richard said soberly, "You cannot dispute what you see for yourself on the chronometer. The capsule *is* going back in time."

They all stared at the silently reversing meter on their individual displays and listened to the voice. 1954... 1953... 1952... 1951... 1950...

Elise closed her eyes briefly. "It's what we've all worked for, for so long now, and heaven forbid that I should dispute it. All we can do is wait and see what happens." She let a small grin escape. "I'd like to remind both of you that we haven't completed the test yet. There's still plenty of time for something to go wrong."

Richard looked over into her wary eyes. "Elise, we've been all over that," he said with respect, measured with a tone of exasperation.

Elise took a deep breath, held it a second, then forced a bleak smile. "You're right, of course. The capsule is traveling back in time. It will go until 1787, where, or when, it will stop and materialize... but in the middle of what? We can control time and location, but tell me, what was happening at any given moment on every location on earth?"

Wende sighed. "I thought that's why we picked the specific time and location we did. There are no records of activity on the date we've chosen," she spoke confidently.

"Besides," Richard argued, "the point is that the past is past. It's already history, and our history has no records of a mysterious time machine suddenly appearing in a crowd." He raised both eyebrows. "The Fermi Paradox?"

"You might have trouble convincing the UFO researchers of that," Elise said.

Richard shrugged. "I know you understand that whatever we are doing has already been done, and we must have succeeded!"

1902... 1901... 1900... 1899... 1898... 1897...

Richard was concerned for Elise as well as for the project. They had been over and over this. All through the project, Elise had exhibited a nagging fear of changing history. She was already recognized as one of the most eminent experts in the United States, if not the world, in the field of resonance frequencies and their application to time travel yet it seemed she still had to convince herself that she was doing the right thing. As for himself, there wasn't the slightest doubt in his mind that time was the only frontier to conquer.

When Richard was a child, and all the other kids were out playing games and being children, he was learning to assemble (and disassemble) and repair clocks and watches. He never seemed to have time to do the things expected of him. Time itself obsessed him. So, it was natural that he ended up working at General Amalgamated.

He had started working after Elise had established herself as the senior researcher. As a technician, he quickly proved his value and was promoted as one of her top assistants on this project. In time, he had grown very fond of her. She was as dedicated to her work as he was. It was their mutual bond. He worried about her fears of changing history, her fear of changing the events of her own birth, and it was a little discomforting to him as well. After all, if she had never been born, where would he be now?

Wende interrupted his rambling thoughts. "We are nearing one hundred years of the projected target. Prepare for reverse thrust."

1885... 1884... 1883... 1882...

The test called for the capsule to materialize just long enough to gather dust that could be laser-radiation dated to authenticate the flight. Proven time travel had unlimited possibilities in all the sciences from anthropology to zoology and every off shoot in-between. Historians were possibly the most interested and excited about it. Right now, a dear old friend of Elise's sat in his university office awaiting a call. Professor Milton Sanford, foremost historian, was among the very few people even aware of today's test.

Or so Elise thought. What she wasn't aware of was the interest of a very select few members of the United States Government Department of Defense. Secretary of Defense Julian Hunter had seen to it that whatever money needed was covertly channeled to the project, and now he eagerly awaited the results.

Wende looked back to her display to prepare for materialization. She was once again tense, but sure of herself. She was a totally dedicated, if somewhat unorganized, technician. Several times, minor delays in the project had been caused by her misplacing research material, but in a pinch, she always came through. Elise had managed to cover for her mistakes each time, which she deeply appreciated, but Wende disliked the uncomfortable feeling it left. She knew that she had the reputation of being the clown, but after this test, everyone would know different. She, Elise, and Richard were making history.

Elise checked various readouts in her display.

1879... 1878...

All concentration was shattered as a small green light suddenly went dark on their holographic displays and a red light began flashing around the entire edge of the display just before large sections went dark. An insistent beeping alarm tone sounded.

"Malfunction!" It was Richard's voice. "Malfunction! Something's wrong."

"Malfunction..." ABBI's calm feminine voice broke in, sounding as calm as it did when calling out the countdown. "Malfunction... malfunction..."

Elise's face turned ashen. Malfunction! It couldn't be. She had quietly convinced herself that the mission would be successful. After all, there were too many failsafe devices built into the system.

"What is it?" she asked in a firm quiet voice as she searched her display for any reason for the malfunction.

"I don't know, but..." Richard's face went white. "My God! I think we have materialization! ABBI, can you confirm?"

"Materialization confirmation," the soft voice said before it continued repeating, "Malfunction..."

All three of them typed furiously on their displays until, as suddenly as their displays had gone dark, they lit back up, but now red and amber lights covered them.

Elise looked at the chronometer. It had stopped at 1876. She glanced over at Wende. "Wende, what do you have?"

"Confirmation of materialization." Wende was strangely calm in the midst of crisis. "Time, 1876. I'm trying to pinpoint the location."

Richard typed furiously on his holographic keyboard attempting to apply full forward time-thrust on the control. "No response," he shouted, "it's stuck in time!" As lights began to turn green, he quickly checked the other functions. Everything showed normal parameters, but the chronometer had stopped, and a single display indicated materialization!

Elise spun in her swivel chair checking each of the readouts on her 360-degree display. Richard was right. Everything coming back showed normal operation except for the two readouts. She bit her lower lip and tasted blood. Something somewhere had to show what was wrong. Something made the chronometer stop. She looked over into Richard's expectant eyes. Now what?

"More forward thrust," she said calmly as she returned to her own display.

Richard's voice trembled with frustration as he tapped on a key repeatedly. "That's all there is. I can't get any more! ABBI, can you gain more forward thrust?"

ABBI's voice calmly informed them, "Maximum thrust is achieved… malfunction… malfunction…"

Elise: "Reverse, then. Slowly."

Richard's shaking finger tapped another program key on the keyboard to initiate reverse thrust.

"Wende, can you tell me where the capsule was?" she snapped.

Wende hesitated before speaking. "I'm not sure." She glanced across her monitor and copied some numbers down on her notepad, then quickly typed on the holographic keyboard in her display. "I think some of my readings are screwed up."

Elise frowned. Screwed up? What kind of a technical description was that supposed to be? She didn't have time for a lecture now, though. She put her mind back to the problem at hand.

Richard had the controls in full reverse. The lights on the display blinked once more, then again. No one spoke, and in the strained quiet, ABBI's voice seemed twice as annoying as before as well as the alarm as they repeated their warning… "Malfunction… malfunction…" Richard looked up at the display. "ABBI, you can stop with the warning now." The voice complied, and the alarm tone stopped.

Seconds trickled by.

Elise's eyes were riveted to the chronometer. Slowly, it began to read out a jerking forward time movement. Elise let her breath go. "It's working! See if you can ease up any on the thrust."

Richard typed the 'slow code' sequence. The chronometer now showed a steady, but slower, movement of gaining years. ABBI's voice started reading off the chronometer readings. "1877… 1878… 1879…

The relief of the moving chronometer allowed some color to return to Elise's face. She slumped in her seat. Malfunction. How? Why? Her mind raced over several possibilities, but nothing seemed immediately feasible. She spun around looking at every display in her 360-degree display, checking each indicator with her own eyes. Wende was busy making notes and entering new information codes into the database on her notepad. Already the process of tracking down the cause of the malfunction was in progress. Once the capsule was safely returned, every component would be gone over with a fine-tooth comb… *if* the capsule was safely returned.

Elise looked over at Richard and Wende. Her mind was in turmoil. "What have we done?" she murmured softly. "What have we done?" No one answered her as the familiar wave of uneasiness about changing time washed over her.

It seemed to be taking forever for the capsule to return. She desperately wanted to tell Richard to go to maximum thrust, but as long as everything was working, there was no reason to push their luck. She kept silent.

All display lights now were back in the green, showing normal operation and they seemed to be holding.

All eyes watched the chronometer on their individual

displays. All minds raced, coming up with possible reasons for a malfunction and filing these reasons away to be checked later. No one spoke. It was as if the silence was all that was keeping the system working, and no one wanted to destroy it.

Elise chewed her lip.

Wende found herself holding her breath again.

Richard wanted to wipe the perspiration from around his eyes, but he was afraid to move his hands hovering above the keyboard.

They all waited impatiently.

CHAPTER 2

It was a hot, dusty afternoon. Above all else, it was dusty. There was a slight southerly breeze, but all it did was blow the hot air and dust around. The sweltering Montana Territory sun beat down unmercifully, burning skin and parching throats. Sparse patches of grass, dried out to a burnished gold, waved gently across the rolling hills.

Captain Chris Garrett stood alone just over a small rise away from the other men. The dust blew in around his collar, leaving grinding grits of sand that irritated his neck, but at least he was alone for a while. He had been with these same men for who cares how many weeks now. He was getting sick of their faces, their idle chatter, their smell. Not that he smelled much better.

He tried to force the business at hand out of his mind. He thought pleasant thoughts like a real bath, sitting in a chair in the shade of the barrack's porch, a real cold drink of anything... but every time he closed his eyes, he saw Indians or soldiers.

He unknotted his bandana from around his throat and wiped his face and neck with it. "Ain't anything more miserable than dust," he told himself.

"Cap'n. Hey, Cap'n!"

Oh, no, now what? He looked down at the ground then turned around slowly and looked up. It was Lieutenant Colonel

Custer's personal aide. He came puffing up to Chris.

"I been lookin' all over for you, sir."

"What is it, soldier?"

"The colonel wants to see you in his tent right away, sir."

Chris winced. He had completely forgotten about the briefing. He told the aide that he would be right there and dismissed him with a crisp salute. The aide trotted off.

Chris adjusted his floppy hat and started down the gentle slope. He wasn't looking forward to this briefing at all.

Lieutenant Colonel George A. Custer was waiting with the other officers when Chris joined them. The colonel snorted with impatience and began talking. Chris listened but didn't really hear what was being said. He had an ominous feeling of dread ever since they had moved into the Montana Territory.

The U.S. Army was in the process of 'rounding up' all the Sioux and Cheyenne Indians in the territory for transfer to reservations. Custer's regiment had joined the expedition under the command of General Terry. Recent treaties called for the transfer, and Terry was following up.

As the troops moved into Montana Territory, scouts had reported that an Indian village lay 'somewhere ahead'. It was about as vague a report as could be expected from Indian scouts. General Terry ordered colonel Custer to find the village. It was an order that Custer took on with relish. Four days later, on June 25, 1876, today, Custer had the village pinpointed about fifteen miles beyond where they now stood. It lay in a small valley along the Little Big Horn River. Custer reckoned there were about one thousand Indians who could easily be rounded up by the six hundred fifty men in his regiment.

Chris took off his bandana, removed his hat, and wiped his forehead as Custer continued speaking.

"Today, we have an opportunity to place our names in the pages of history for all time. As you know, just ahead is our objective. General Terry has ordered that we should round up all Indians in and about that village, and damn it, that's what we're going to do!" He slammed a fist into an open palm, causing dust to rise from his sleeve.

Indians. It must have been a slip of the tongue. That was the first time Chris had ever heard Custer use that name. It was always 'red devils', or 'worthless savages', or some such. But never 'Indians'.

Rounding up Indians to be placed on a reservation was one thing, but 'golden-haired' Custer had a reputation as an Indian fighter, the 'protector of all that is good and right'. Rounding up Indians wasn't in Custer's private book of military action. Chris just hoped nothing came of it. Still, he was uneasy.

Custer turned his attention to one of Chris' companions. "Captain Benteen, you'll take two hundred men, you'll be column A, and circle off here to our left. I want you to search every little valley, and I mean every one, Captain. Leave no stone unturned. Believe me, those wily devils can hide in places where you can't even see ground cover."

Benteen nodded.

"You'll round them up and drive them down to the river, here, near the village." Custer pointed to his map. "If you meet any resistance, well, you know what to do." His face was hard.

"Yes, sir."

Chris looked at Captain Frederick W. Benteen. About his own age, dressed in the same dust covered uniform as Chris, but there was one big difference between them. Benteen was scared of what was coming, and Chris wasn't. You couldn't miss the look of relief on Benteen's face when he learned that he wouldn't be going directly into the village. Captain Benteen wasn't a coward. He had just been around Custer for a while and knew that Custer always went beyond simple orders. 'Rounding up' could easily escalate into a massacre.

"There are only about a thousand savages in the entire area," Custer said, "and I expect most of them to be in the camp. You'll be looking for any stray hunting parties. I don't want any of them to get away. Is that understood?"

Captain Benteen nodded excitedly. "I think, though, sir, that if I were to head off more here, to the west," he pointed to the well-worn map, "I could cover more area."

Custer studied the map and listened to Benteen. Chris' mind began to wander. He wanted a bath. He wanted something cold to drink. He wanted to go home, wherever that was. But as he thought of it more, the army *was* his home. He was a career man, having risen through the ranks. He didn't have any family left after the Civil War, at least none that he knew of. He had joined the army as soon as he was old enough and he enjoyed it. He liked the discipline, the training, and the long hard rides that are a part of cavalry life.

Chris was a natural athlete, a quick learner, and a born leader. He was promoted quickly without offending fellow soldiers since everyone had deep respect for him. Custer was rapidly building himself a reputation as an Indian fighter, having been promoted to the rank of Brigadier General of Volunteers during the Civil War, and Chris originally looked forward to being assigned to his regiment. Custer promoted Chris to Captain in short order, but Chris' attitude towards the now Lieutenant Colonel had begun to sour by this point in time.

Generally, an exercise of this type, rounding up Indians, wouldn't mean much to Chris, but something was different this time. He could feel it in his bones. He sensed the other men had their hackles up, too. There was a tension in the dry air that had everyone edgy. Normally, Chris wouldn't feel the need to be alone, but something was up, and he needed to think about it.

"And you, Chris," Custer's booming voice brought Chris back. "You'll be column B. You'll have two hundred and fifty men."

Chris raised his eyebrows but said nothing. Why was he going to have the larger group?

"I like Fred's idea about swinging wider to the West. I'll do the same to the East. I can't imagine that you'll have very much trouble in the village itself. You'll certainly have the advantage of surprise." He chuckled loudly.

Chris was confused. He had assumed that Custer would lead the main force. He looked at his commander, surprise in his eyes.

"Something wrong, Chris?"

Chris still had his bandana in his hand. He wiped the back of his neck with it before he spoke. "No, nothing's wrong. I was just assuming that you would lead the main force into the village."

Custer was mildly amused. "The heat is getting to you, Chris. Think, now. Why would I send two columns to the flanks?"

Chris shook his head. "I understand that..." his voice trailed off. Something didn't feel right. What did the Colonel know that he wasn't telling the rest of them? If there were only a few stray hunting parties outside of the village, then why use four hundred men to round them up? And why didn't Custer want the glory of leading the main force? If the scout's information was reliable, there would be no need for such large diversionary columns.

Chris knew that Sitting Bull had vowed he would never go to the reservations. Chris had visions of all the tribes uniting against the white soldiers. He stared at Custer. Was this what the Colonel counting on?

"Something wrong, Chris? I thought you would be eager to lead the main attack. This is your big chance to make a name for yourself."

Attack? Strong language for a 'round up' Chris thought. Yes, something was wrong. Custer's attitude towards this whole campaign was wrong. Chris shifted his weight to his other foot. Maybe it was just the heat and the dust. The heavy blue uniform didn't make things any more comfortable either.

"You're mighty quiet, Chris. What's worryin' you? There are only a thousand of them red devils in the whole area. All the scouts are reporting the same thing. You'll be riding into that village with complete surprise, and Fred and I will be right behind you on the flanks." Chris' eyes hardened. "There's nothing to be afraid of. This isn't like you." Colonel Custer was clearly agitated with Chris' hesitancy.

Chris lowered his eyes and swallowed hard to keep from saying what his mind was trying to sort out. "Sorry, sir." Afraid? No, it wasn't fear that bothered him. He couldn't put it exactly into words, but something nagged at him like a bad dream he couldn't completely remember or completely forget. He stared out across the rolling hills. The sparse dried grasses waved stiffly back and forth in the breeze. The dark Montana soil shimmered in the heat. Just off in the distance lay the Indian village, near the river.

Things would be a little greener by the river; greener and cooler. He tried to picture the village. The buffalo hide teepees would be set on the banks of the river. Indian children were most likely playing in the water to ward off the intense heat. He could see the women bustling about, busy with their daily chores, cooking, preparing skins for clothing for the coming winter. The men would either be out hunting or working on their weapons. He imagined a hot day like this to be somewhat lackadaisical. The Indians would have many things on their minds, but certainly not an attack by Golden Hair Custer. A single word appeared in Chris' mind: Slaughter.

"If you don't mind joining us, Captain Garrett, you might want to get your gear and your men together." Custer's voice was hard. "Dismissed!" He turned sharply and marched away.

Benteen touched Chris' arm. "I feel it, too," he said, then turned and walked towards the troops.

Chris looked after Benteen. He had to get away for a few minutes. He had to think by himself, sort things out, get his priorities in order. He shifted his long-bladed officer's sword around his side and turned towards the small rise he had been behind earlier. He waited a moment, making sure no one was paying him any mind, then strode smartly over the rise. Five minutes alone were all he needed. Once out of sight, he stopped, closed his eyes and listened. The troops were preparing their equipment, their horses, and their rifles.

Chris sighed deeply.

He wasn't aware of the sudden rippling movement in the

air next to him, touching him. He never saw the capsule appear. He just stood there, hands clasped behind his back, wishing he didn't have to participate in this ugly mess. When the capsule immediately began to dematerialize, taking him with it, he didn't even realize he was getting his wish.

CHAPTER 3

No one in the room spoke. An electrifying chill swept the air as ABBI's voice softly and calmly called off the years. All eyes were glued to their display chronometers as it was a visible link to the capsule's progress to the present, confirming the computer voice.

1880... 1881... 1882... 1883... 1884...

The calm feminine voice was softly reciting the numbers as all systems settled back into normal function. The damned computer acted as though nothing had gone wrong at all. But then, computers are like that, Elise thought. She suddenly stuck her hands in her lab coat pockets and laughed, her voice sounding strangely relieved.

Richard, puzzled but afraid to take his eyes from the chronometer, asked, "What is funny at a time like this?"

Elise threw her head back, her eyes closed. "Don't you see, Richard? You were right, but for the wrong reasons."

He scrunched up his face. "What are you talking about?"

"You said there was nothing to be afraid about, and you were right. Only you said we were a success because we didn't interrupt whatever was going on over two hundred years ago, and there you were wrong. We didn't interrupt whatever was going on two hundred years ago because we never made it back two hundred years." She laughed again. "History books don't show us because we failed."

Richard didn't quite see the humor in Elise's logic, but he didn't comment.

1944... 1945... 1946... 1947...

All systems on the displays maintained normal function. Richard carefully typed in a sequence of code. He was as anxious as Elise to bring the capsule back before there was another malfunction.

1977... 1978... 1979... 1980... 1981...

Wende turned around in her display checking readouts from every angle. The most critical part of the test was coming up. Timing was everything during materialization. A second too soon or too late could cause a miss in time of months. It was up to Wende to coordinate the timing phase. Wende had a small reputation as a scatterbrain, but her one saving grace was her ability to come through in a crisis. She was perfectly calm now.

"Appearance phase coming up, Richard." Now that the mission had aborted, Wende wanted the capsule back in the right time slot on the first try.

2037... 2038... 2039... 2040...

"Five years, Phase One," she called out over ABBI's voice.

Richard was ready and typed the coded instructions on his keyboard. He also slowed the capsule's return rate. ABBI's voice responded correspondingly.

"Phase Two," Wende called out.

Richard typed quickly, repeating his last two actions as he would for each phase of Appearance.

"Phase Three... Phase Four..."

Elise switched her monitor back to the capsule display. She wanted to observe materialization.

"Phase Five, stand by."

Richard typed in the last coded sequence, stopped the capsule return rate, and held a trembling finger over the key to initiate materialization.

"Initiate materialization!" Wende stepped towards Elise's cubicle display hoping to witness the capsule's return.

Richard tapped his finger firmly on the keyboard and then

he too, turned to see if he could see anything on Elise's display. He couldn't really see through his own display and Elise's at the same time, but he would know if they were successful by her reaction.

As on water, the currents of air began a rippling movement, and the vague outline of the capsule began to manifest itself. Iridescent colors swirled into coalescence and in less than twelve seconds, complete materialization had occurred. The capsule was intact, but there were no grateful sighs of relief... only ABBI's reassuring voice, "Materialization complete. Program complete. Congratulations., Doctor McAllister."

Richard couldn't figure out Elise and Wende's blank stares. Now what? He and Wende both moved to Elise's cubicle, took one look at the display, and Richard's mouth dropped open in a most ungentlemanly manner.

Elise was the first to recover from the shock. She breathed out a quiet "My God!" then took stock of what confronted them.

Standing next to the capsule, apparently completely unaware of his surroundings, was a man. He was dressed in a grubby-looking, dusty blue uniform. Its brass buttons had long ago lost their luster and the gold braid on his shoulder was brown with dirt. The whole uniform, indeed, the whole man was covered with dust. He was wearing tall black boots with his pants tucked inside the tops. Around his waist was a wide black belt that held a pistol in a leather holster on one side, and a long sword scabbard on his other side.

He stood unconcerned, his hands clasped behind his back, his head up, eyes closed, looking as though he might be lost in a daydream; perhaps dreaming that he was somewhere else.

Elise was also dimly aware of his rugged handsomeness. The coarse build of his muscular body was unmistakable even through the heavy uniform. Only the floppy hat on his head detracted from his perfect looks.

Wende began to come out of her trance. "Look at that! Tell me I'm seeing what I'm seeing... or better yet, tell me I'm not seeing what I'm seeing!"

"I see it," Richard mumbled, "but I sure don't believe it. We picked up a hitch hiker somewhere along the way, and that just can't be."

"We've got to send him back! Back to your posts! ABBI, where did he come from?"

ABBI responded, "Insufficient data. Program complete."

Wende and Richard looked at Elise at the same time. She felt lightheaded. It was her worst fears come true. Like a terrible nightmare, they had interrupted history and brought a person into the future. She had tried to prepare herself mentally in the last few weeks for the event of a failure, but this... nothing could have prepared her for this shock. Her unscientific, panicky thought was that he had to be put back immediately!

Wende stared at the figure on the monitor. He looked to be an army officer of some sort. He was magnificent. She smiled, then frowned. "Send him back? Where? Why? Don't you realize what we've got here?"

Richard saw the struggling agony in Elise's face. "We can't send him back. We don't know where he's from first of all, and we don't even know how we brought him here."

"The capsule," Elise mumbled.

"We can't use the capsule again until we find out what caused the malfunction in the first place. If we tried to use it again, we might kill him."

"But that could take days, weeks," Elise snapped. "We've got to send him back this minute. We may even be too late already. We have to..."

"We can't."

Elise sagged against the cubicle wall and stared at the floating monitor. The man was obviously totally unaware that he was anywhere other than where he was when he closed his eyes. If they could send him back before he realized anything was wrong... "Richard, we've got..."

Richard stopped her. "I'm sorry, but you know as well as I do that there's nothing we can do. We're going to have to make

corrections in the system before we can attempt another shot."
His heart really hurt for the fear showing in Elise's face. "We
may as well accept what's happened and begin our corrections.
We'll have to quarantine him until we figure out what went
wrong. It's the best we can do for him." He knew what she
must be going through, but he also knew the ramifications of
returning their unaware guest, and he held his ground.

Wende was agitated. "We've got the chance of a lifetime
standing right in the other room, and you want to send him
back? That's ridiculous. We've got to find out who he is.
Richard, talk to him."

Richard hesitated, then hesitantly pushed a key.

"No, Richard." Elise reached over and put her hand on his
arm. "I'll do it."

He looked up into her eyes and saw her determination to
meet the situation head on. Her whole face changed as she set
her jaw. She was in control of herself again. She cleared her
throat, keyed her mic and spoke as calmly as she could under
the circumstances.

"This is Doctor Elise McAllister. Can you hear me?"

Chris Garrett was reveling in a glorious daydream. He was
somewhere far away from the Montana Territory. It was a cool,
calm place. In fact, he actually felt cooler. Then suddenly, he
heard a voice breaking into his dream. No, he wasn't ready to
return to reality yet. The distant voice became distinct.

"This is Doctor Elise McAllister. Can you hear me?"

Chris didn't open his eyes, but he did frown. Sounded like a
female voice. He was obviously hearing voices as part of his
very realistic daydream.

"What is your name?"

There it was again. The sun. It must be the sun. That was a
good explanation. The heat was playing a little trick on him. He
smiled. He was in good physical shape and a little heat wasn't
going to get the best of him.

"Can you hear me? What is your name?"

"Chris Garrett," he said, chuckling. "Captain Chris Garrett, U.S. Army, Cavalry. I'm not that crazy yet."

"Captain Garrett, this is Doctor Elise McAllister. How do you feel?"

Chris closed his eyes even tighter and frowned again. Something was wrong. Daydreams weren't supposed to talk back. At least he didn't think they were... not out loud, at least.

"Captain Garrett, can you hear me? Are you all right? How do you feel?"

Chris' voice cracked a little when he finally spoke. "Who did you say you were?"

"This is Doctor Elise McAllister."

Doctor? Chris slowly squinted through one eyelid. What was going on? Where was he? His eyes inched around in their sockets, and he surveyed his surroundings. What he saw definitely was not the Montana Territory hills that he was standing on... should have been standing on. He was in an unbelievably white room. He closed his eye, then squinted through both eyes. Nope... he was in a room of some sort. The walls were bare. There were no windows. Light emitted from box shapes in the ceiling. He was standing next to a... he never knew what because at that moment his vision blurred, and his head began to swim. He pushed his hat back and wiped his forehead with his hand, and then his knees buckled.

Elise cried out as she watched the figure suddenly slump to the floor. "Quick, let's get in to him! The shock of molecular transfer may have been too much of a strain on his biological system." She quickly led the way to the resonance chamber.

The chamber was approximately twelve feet square. The walls were made of two thin layers of a special alloy with a vacuum space between each layer. The room was bare except for a platform for the small capsule in the center of the floor. The ceiling contained two overhead lights, each with a reformulated protective shield. There were no windows. Two walls held large resonance monitors. One wall had an opening for the lens of the closed-circuit digital camera. The fourth wall had the chamber door.

Elise quickly undid the latches on the door and broke the seal. Pushing the door inward, there was a rush of air. Protocols of dust confinement were abandoned as she rushed over to the fallen Captain Garrett. Richard and Wende were close on her heels. Elise knelt down and touched his throat looking for a carotid pulse.

Richard asked breathlessly. "Is he...?"

"No, he's got a pulse. He's just unconscious. Let's move him to the anteroom. We'll lay him on the couch in there."

Richard straddled the captain intending to pick him up and carry him to the anteroom. He grabbed an arm and pulled. All that came up was the arm. "He's kind of heavy," Richard mumbled. He knelt down, put one arm under Chris' back and one arm under his legs, and strained to lift. Nothing happened.

Wende had to smile in spite of herself and the circumstances. Richard tried two more feeble attempts at lifting the captain, resulting only in a red face from the exertion.

"Instead of standing there laughing," Richard sputtered indignantly, "you might try helping me."

"I'm sorry. It's just that you look so... unsubstantial trying to lift that hunk of man by yourself." She bent down to help him. Elise grabbed hold too, and between the three of them, they were able to move the unconscious figure out of the test chamber.

Wende coughed. "When is the last time this guy took a bath?"

Elise had never seen anyone like him. She thought he must weigh a ton, but there was no denying it must be all muscle. From the way he looked and smelled, he obviously had been out riding a horse for a while, but there was no horse here. Was the molecular transfer system somehow selective? Could only certain molecules be accelerated? There were so many questions, and this man held the answers, yet Elise knew he would be able to tell them nothing. They staggered through the lab, past Elise's office, and out into the anteroom, laying Chris as gently as they could on the couch. No one had conceived of a man being brought back, so no preparations had been made for this eventuality.

Wende got a paper towel, wet it in the sink against one wall, and placed it on the man's forehead. She stared at him like she had never seen a man before. He was beautiful.

"Does he have any identification?" Richard asked, "driver's license, credit card, anything?"

Elise looked at Richard. "Richard, we've just brought him from the year 1876. That's, what, a hundred and sixty-nine years ago!"

Wende frowned. "He was probably too young to drive back then, huh?" she teased Richard.

Richard was embarrassed. "Well, you know what I mean..."

Elise went through each of Chris' pockets. "Nothing," she reported. "All we've got is his name, Captain Chris Garrett, and the fact that he belonged to the U.S. Army Cavalry in 1876." She thought for a moment before speaking again. "Wende, can you go figure out what day we picked him up?"

Wende nodded. "If everything isn't screwed up too bad, ABBI should have it. I can track back and find the date. I could probably extrapolate the exact time."

Elise rolled her eyes. "I know how it's done. I want you to go do it... and I don't care what time, just the date. I can call Professor Sanford at the university. If anybody can identify our mystery man, he can."

Richard pursed his lips. "Do you suppose it's wise to let this out yet? After all, he isn't supposed to be here."

"I don't intend to let anything out. The Professor is a very close friend of mine. I ask him these kinds of questions all the time. For all he needs to know, I'm working on another paper." She looked at Wende and spoke with a sharp tone. "The date? I can't call until I have it."

Wende hurried out of the room.

Elise sat on the edge of the couch next to the unmoving

Captain. She gazed at the prostrate figure, trouble back in her eyes. "Richard, what have I done?"

"What we have done," Richard said, emphasizing the 'we', "could not have been prevented. Some things are just out of our hands. There's no way to even begin to guess at what went wrong until we can check the programs and data. This whole experiment is so theoretical, the malfunction may not even be with our computers."

There were tears in Elises' eyes. "I checked everything myself before the test and it all checked out perfectly."

"And I checked it, and so did Wende. That's what I'm saying. There are so many unknown variables in the time frontier, the mistake probably isn't in what we did, but what we didn't know."

"Mistake. I'm so afraid that's what we've done.... made a huge mistake." A tear slid down her cheek.

Richard sat down beside her and put his arms around her. "Look, we're all tired. Tension is high because we failed and it's an emotional time. Try to calm down."

Elise put her head on Richard's shoulder. "But I checked everything myself…"

"Shhhhh," Richard quieted her. "It doesn't matter now, and it won't matter in a hundred years. All we can do is pick up and go on with what we have."

"And what about him?"

"We'll deal with him as quickly and quietly as we can."

Elise sighed. "You're right, of course." She wiped her eyes. "There's no use crying over spilled milk."

"Exactly."

"Then why do I feel like such a failure? To myself and to him."

"Because you're a person who cares very deeply about the lives of other people… and I'm grateful for that." He hugged her again.

"Here's the data…" Wende rushed into the room but came up short when she saw Elise in Richard's arms. "… Doctor."

Elises' face flushed and she quickly stood to take the data sheet from Wende.

Point of materialization was June 25, 1876. It meant nothing to Elise, but her brain felt numb anyway. "I'll be right back," she said. "Keep an eye on our friend."

She used ABBI in her office to call the Professor. "Professor, this is Elise."

The Professor's voice boomed. "Elise! The test, have you completed it? Was it a success? Tell me, girl, don't keep an old man in suspense. It's not good for my heart."

Elise felt guilty about lying to her friend, but she knew she had to... and it wasn't all a lie. "I'm afraid the test was a failure. We had a malfunction. We're checking it out now." She could hear the disappointment in his silence. "I'm sorry." She heard his chair squeak after a moment.

"I'm sorry, too," he said after a pause. "I guess I shouldn't have gotten myself so worked up about it."

"Professor, as long as I have you on the tel, I need some help." She could picture the old man sitting at his massive desk, surrounded by books. He wasn't a big man physically and his office seemed to dwarf him. Elise was a frequent visitor to the office seeking bits and pieces of information for various papers she published, but she never got used to the utter disarray of the room. Books covered everything, and the books were covered with dust. The Professor didn't feel that he had time to waste on such trivial matters as cleaning, although he was personally immaculate. Elise was always amazed at the sheer number of books and the fact that no matter what she asked him, he never really had to refer to any of the volumes. The total knowledge contained in these books was also stored in the Professor's mind. He was, to say the least, amazing.

"Help?" His voice was brighter. "Does it have anything to do with the test?"

Elise winced. "Well... not exactly..." She felt terrible. "It's just some information I need for a paper."

"The test is barely over and you're working on a paper?

Curious. And it has nothing to do with the test?"

Elise bit her lip and tried to sound flippant. "No, I'm afraid not. Richard and Wende are reviewing the test to see what went wrong. Something happened before we really got started."

"All right. What do you need?"

Elise hesitated. "I'm looking for some information on a man."

The Professor was taken by surprise. "A man? Ten minutes after testing the world's first time travel vehicle, you want information on a man? Elise, you've got your whole life to worry about men."

She tried to laugh. "The test was almost an hour ago. Now, I'm talking about a historical figure. Someone who's been..." She caught herself just in time. She had almost told him, and while she had enormous respect for her friend, it just wasn't time to reveal the captain's presence yet... if ever. "We have a few things to go on." She paused, not sure how to proceed. "It's very important."

The professor was dying of curiosity now, but he paused, thinking. Elise could picture him stroking his finely trimmed beard. He always did that when he was thinking.

"All right, what do you have?"

"His name is Captain Chris Garrett."

The Professor was puzzled. "Let me see if I have this straight. You want me to tell you who a certain historical figure is, that you already know who he is?"

"He's... was... a cavalry officer in the U.S. Army in 1876, but that's all we know about him."

"So, what else do you need to know?"

Elise took a deep breath. "What was he doing on June 25, 1876?" She knew what his immediate reaction would be. She had spent enough time with him to know. He would scrunch up his face, take a piece of hard candy from his left pocket, unwrap it, drop the wrapper on the floor, and pop the candy in his mouth.

An interminable amount of time seemed to pass as the

Professor did indeed do all those things. At length he announced, "Captain Chris Garrett."

Elise heard him playing with the candy in his mouth. She wished he would hurry up. The captain might come to at any minute.

"I can tell you what you want to know about Captain Garrett without even looking it up, although the book is right here somewhere... I think."

She heard him rummaging around his desktop. "That's all right, Professor, I may need the book later for authentication, but right now I just need the information. Please?"

"Yes, of course. I'm really surprised you don't recognize the significance of that date yourself. June 25, 1876." He paused to enjoy his candy. "I think I can safely assure you that Captain Garrett was in the Montana Territory, as it was called then, on that day. In fact, he was near the Little Big Horn River."

Elise gasped. The Little Big Horn River, of course! Custer's last stand! Color drained from her face; panic gripped her. "Captain Garrett was in the battle of the Little Big Horn?" Her heart began to thump wildly, loudly. She knew that 1876 was the year of the big Indian campaign. If Captain Garrett had been plucked right out of the middle of the battle of the Little Big Horn... oh, God, what had she done? She bit her lip and clenched her fists.

"No," the Professor said, "the captain wasn't in the battle. At least that's the best guess." He sucked the candy in his mouth furiously. "Although he must have been right near it someplace. Actually, there's only a lot of speculation on exactly what did happen to him."

Now it was Elise's turn to be surprised. "What do you mean?" she said, her voice trembling.

"I'm afraid I can only tell you about the speculation. No real facts. Oh, there's the book over there." He abruptly stopped talking and crossed the room.

Elise impatiently closed her eyes. Captain Garrett never made the battle?

"Here we go," said the Professor, sputtering as he blew dust off the book's cover. "It seems Captain Garrett deserted before the actual fighting took place. He was under orders to lead a column of men on an attack directly into the village of Chief Sitting Bull. Apparently, for whatever reasons, it was too much for him to handle and he simply disappeared. Over the hill, as they say. Custer had to call in Major Marcus Reno to take charge of Garrett's command. Captain Garrett never turned up, so he was dishonorably discharged from the army and his name was forever disgraced. Too bad, too. It seems he was a real go-getter before that. Quite a fellow, but I guess we all have our weak moments."

"What have I done?" Elise mumbled vacantly as she slowly sat down in her chair.

"How's that?" Professor Sanford asked.

Elise snapped to. "Oh, nothing, Professor, thanks a lot. You've been a big help as always. I've got to go, so I'll talk to you later."

There was an awkward silence, then the Professor said, "Sure, my dear. You're perfectly welcome."

"Good-bye." Elise signed off.

Professor Sanford closed his pocket tel. "There's something odd going on here," he said to himself, "damned odd."

Elise sat for a moment and tears welled up in her eyes. In a way, she was relieved that Richard was right. They did not interrupt the past. Captain Garrett's disappearance was in the history books, but still she cried for what she had done to him. Accounted for in history books or not, she had caused his disappearance. She took a tissue and wiped her eyes. Whatever had happened, it was now time to confront the captain.

Wende and Richard were still sitting with the unconscious Captain Garrett when Elise entered the anteroom.

"How is he?" Elise asked, anxious to know if he had awakened yet.

"He's still out," Wende told her. "He's been stirring some the last few minutes, though. I think he's starting to come out of it."

"What did you find out?" Richard asked.

Elise shook her head. "It seems our Captain acquired himself quite a reputation on our account."

Wende was puzzled. "What do you mean?"

"Mmmbf. Umbumderuff..." The man startled them all with his sudden mumbling. "Where... ummmbf..."

Elise knelt down beside the couch. "He's coming around." Wende and Richard hovered nearby.

"History in the making!" Wende said, clearly elated. She watched as Chris' eyelids began to flutter.

Richard stood wide-eyed, waiting for the first words from a man who lived a hundred and sixty-nine years ago.

Chris could hear voices as he struggled to wake from his unconscious state. The first thing he saw when he opened his heavy eyelids was Elise's face; at first fuzzily, then as his head cleared, he saw her in focus. Her shining dark hair fell across her round face, framing her large brown eyes. Her white lab coat seemed to have a fuzzy glow around it with the bright lights behind it.

"An angel," Chris said, "I've died and gone to heaven, and you're an angel." He looked at her closely. "You're beautiful. I always figured angels would be beautiful... and you are." He lay back, smiling, and closed his eyes.

Elise blushed. "My name is Doctor Elise McAllister." She watched his face closely as he frowned, thinking.

McAllister... McAllister... that name sounded vaguely familiar to Chris. "Of course! I heard someone calling your name just before I was killed." He opened his eyes. "You're not the Death Angel! You're dressed in white." He took a deep breath. "How did I die?" He closed his eyes again.

Wende and Richard smiled at each other.

"I'm not an angel, and you're not dead," Elise told him. "Look at me."

Chris looked at her. "I'm not dead?" he said, surprised. He fought to remember. "Wait a minute. You said something about

a doctor..." He looked around and saw Richard standing
behind Elise. "You must be the doctor. Then I must be in a
hospital." He lay back on the couch and closed his eyes once
more. "Give it to me straight, Doc. Am I gonna die?"

Richard smiled. "No, you're not going to die."

"Was it an Indian?"

"Was what an Indian?"

"That shot me. Was it an arrow or a rifle?"

"You're not shot."

Chris opened his eyes. "I'm not shot?"

Richard shook his head. Chris looked up at Elise. "I'm not
shot?" Elise shook her head. Chris sat up and looked at Wende.
She shook her head, too. Chris fell back on the couch. "My
God! I've been stabbed!" He began frantically feeling for the
wound, even checking for his scalp. "He must have snuck up
behind me. Have I lost much blood? I feel kind of weak."

"You're not bleeding," Elise told him. "You're not hurt at
all."

"Don't be silly, nurse," Chris snapped, "of course I'm hurt.
I'm in a hospital, aren't I?"

Elise shook her head again.

Chris was getting angry. "Doctor, I demand that you
remove this woman and get someone who will attend to my
wounds!"

Richard stepped forward. "I'm not the doctor."

"What! I should have known. Get me the doctor!"

"Captain Garrett!" Elise's voice was biting. "I *am* the
doctor, and you are not wounded."

Chris stared intently at Elise, then Richard, and Wende. He
sat up again and his eyes traveled slowly around the room. He
didn't recognize anything. It was a small room, perhaps twelve
by fifteen feet. There were two doors leading through opposite
walls.

Against one wall was a row of metal lockers and a small
sink with a mirror above it. Against the wall where he sat was
just the plain couch. A large LED light illuminated the room. It

was, to our standards, a very plain room. To Chris Garrett, it was unbelievable. The sink and lockers were hard enough to try to figure out, but the light source was totally incomprehensible. For a gas lamp, it sure didn't flicker much, and it was so bright. His eyes finally settled back on Elise. "I'm not wounded," he said.

Elise shook her head.

Chris took out his bandana and wiped his face. It was cool in the room, but he was sweating anyway. Funny, he hadn't noticed it before... for a hot, dusty Montana Territory summer day, it was sure cool in this room. "I'm not wounded. You're a woman doctor, and I'm not in a hospital."

Elise was relieved that he was beginning to understand. There was no telling what he might do... no way to gauge his reactions.

Chris smiled. "I've gone loco. That's it, isn't it? I've gone to seed." He lay back and closed his eyes once more. You could always comprehend a situation if only you stayed calm and thought it out. He had been in a couple of tight situations before, and by staying calm, he came out without a scratch. It worried him that he was able to think so clearly when he was crazy, but maybe that's what being crazy was. He had never been crazy before. It sure explained a lot of things, though.

Elise put her hand to her forehead. "You're not crazy." But you're starting to drive me there, she thought.

Chris suddenly sat up and put his feet on the floor. He stood up unsteadily and walked slowly to the mirror. The mirror reflected an image that was sharp and clear unlike any other mirror he had ever seen. He stared at the reflection, intently for a minute, then began to feel his face with his calloused right hand. "Nose. Eyes. Mouth." He smiled awkwardly. "Teeth." After careful investigation, he announced, "Yep, it's me all right."

Elise watched him carefully. "What's the last thing you remember?"

Chris stared at his reflection, watching his mouth move as

he spoke. "The last thing I remember." He thought for a moment, then frowned. "I don't remember the last thing I remember." He closed his eyes and leaned against the sink.

"Do you remember your name?" Richard asked.

"Of course, I do. Chris Garrett… right?"

"You're in the military?"

"Captain, U.S. Army." He stood up almost at attention. He was proud of his rank. "Presently attached to Lieutenant Colonel Custer's regiment in the Montana Territory." His eyes narrowed as he suddenly wondered if he was giving away too much information.

"What year is it?"

Chris turned to face Richard. "Don't you know?"

"What year is it?" Richard insisted.

"It's 1876. Look, I'm not crazy. I don't know what is going on, but I do know who I am, I know how old I am, I know where I am… I mean where I was…" He looked at the three strangers staring at him and felt weak. "Where am I?" He looked near panic.

Elise felt an intense compassion for the man standing before them. He was lost, completely out of his element, and it was all her fault. Her greatest worry was now explaining to him what had happened, where he was, and preserving his sanity when he finally understood; not a task she was eager to start. "Captain Garrett, I think you had best sit down." She motioned to the couch.

Chris walked cautiously to where the three were standing and looked at each of their faces as he sat down. Elise sat next to him on the edge of the cushion. She wanted to throw her arms around him, comfort him and tell him that it was all her fault, but she merely said, "Captain Garrett, supposing I told you that it is no longer 1876."

"Right now, I'd believe just about anything. I've been unconscious for six months? That's a long time."

Elise locked her eyes to his, his face intensely serious. "Suppose I told you that it is now 2045."

Chris looked at her. "Suppose you told me what is twenty forty-five?"

Elise continued trying to keep her voice steady and calm. "The year. Two thousand and forty-five. Suppose I told you that you had been brought into the future, a hundred and sixty-nine years into the future, due to a malfunction in a time travel vehicle." Elise studied his face carefully for a reaction.

Chris frowned. "What?" His voice was a bit shaky. He paused as though thinking about what she had said. "Not 1876?" He frowned again. "I didn't say I'd believe everything you tell me," he said, forming his words carefully. "Truth is, I don't even know what you just said and I'm having a lot of trouble swallowing any of it. I think you're loco." He stood up abruptly.

"We don't expect you to take everything we say at face value right off," Richard said, "but look around you. How many things do you recognize?" He moved over to the sink and turned on the water. "Running water?" He moved to the light switch near the door and flicked it off, then right back on. "Electric lights? Are these things from your time, Captain?"

Chris stared in amazement, speechless. Never did his eyes behold such things. "Do that again." He pointed at the lights.

Richard switched them off and on again. "Not your average 1876 household items, eh, Captain?"

"Captain, please sit down and let us explain," Elise said quietly.

Chris shook his head. He was a man used to making quick decisions, and although his head was beginning to throb, now was the time for a decision. "I think maybe I'd like to go outside and find out just for myself where I am."

Richard stepped forward. "Captain Garrett, I assure you..."

He didn't get to finish his sentence. Chris drew his revolver and pointed it at Richard and Wende. "I think you two had better sit down next to your friend." Chris pointed to the couch.

They did.

"I don't know what's going on here," Chris said, "but I

intend to find out. I think it would be best if you stayed right here and didn't try to follow me. If I find out what you're saying is true, and I know it isn't, I'll come back."

Elise knew she mustn't let him go outside. Besides the fact that only Richard, Wende, and herself knew of his existence, Captain Garrett was in no way prepared for the world outside. Elise feared that he was in a highly unstable mental state… who wouldn't be?

"Captain Garrett don't be a fool," she said. "You're not prepared to go outside this room, much less this building. We are trying to help you."

Chris' head began to spin. He tried to shake it off.

"Please, Captain," Elise pleaded, "let us help." She stood and took a step towards Chris.

"No." He pointed the pistol directly at Elise. "I'll take my chances. Colonel Custer is bound to be looking for me."

"Colonel Custer?" Richard exclaimed.

Elise stared coldly into Chris' eyes. "Colonel Custer is dead," she said.

Chris stopped. The whole room was spinning now, and he was having a difficult time standing.

"He's been dead for over one hundred years." Elise could see that Chris was about to fall. "Please, Captain…"

Chris looked into those beautiful brown eyes. "Colonel Custer…" He slumped to the floor, the gun slipping from his fingers.

"Quick, get him back to the couch," Elise cried.

Richard and Wende jumped to help.

"Now what are we going to do?" Wende asked.

Richard unbuckled Chris' holster and scabbard belt. "First things first. We take away his weapons." He struggled to lift the belt. "Good Lord, he carried these things around all day?" After he disarmed the captain, the three lifted him up and laid him down on the couch. Elise checked his pulse and found it to be strong and regular.

"So, now what do we do?" Wende asked again.

Elise looked at her watch. "I've got to call Dr. Bruce. I'm surprised that he hasn't called here already. We're way behind schedule. Wende, you and Richard start checking the program data. We've got to trace the cause of the malfunction."

"What about our friend," Richard asked.

"Let him sleep," Elise said. "We'll keep an eye on him to make sure he doesn't try to leave."

"Are you going to tell Dr. Bruce about him?"

Elise frowned. "Not yet. Maybe we can still send him back."

"Maybe we're not supposed to send him back," Richard said with a little more force to his voice than he intended.

"Let's go to work," was her reply.

Elise really didn't want to call Dr. Bruce. She had never met the man; not once in the entire time she had worked at General Amalgamated Labs. She had, of course, seen his picture and had talked to him on the tel, but she had never seen him in person. Dr. Bruce was legendary in the scientific world. He had founded General Amalgamated, made many unbelievable discoveries and achievements here, but then a few years ago had abruptly turned over all work to a variety of scientists, and had never been seen around the labs again. He stayed locked up in his own office high atop the building. Rumor was he had also turned it into his residence as well. None of his current crop of scientists had ever met him in person; however, each department head was directly responsible to him and so was in contact exclusively by tel or text. By listening to his thunderous voice over the tel, Elise had pictured his personality as you might picture any tyrant. She hesitantly had ABBI connect privately to his office. He answered immediately.

"Dr. Bruce, this is Elise McAllister."

"McAllister! What the hell is going on down there? You should have completed the test sixteen minutes ago. I've got a room full of press outside of my office!"

"Press?" When it rains, it pours, Elise thought. "Dr. Bruce, I'm afraid I have some rather bad news to report."

There was a slight pause. "Bad news?" It was odd how his voice could sound almost pleasant at the strangest times. "Bad news?" he repeated softly.

Elise cringed. "Yes, sir. I'm afraid we had a malfunction. We've been working, checking it out. I wanted to find the cause before I called you…"

"And?"

"And it's too early to tell. We haven't found anything yet."

"What happened?" His voice was suddenly, strangely calm.

Elise took a sharp breath. "What do you mean, what happened?" He couldn't possibly know about the captain.

"What was the malfunction? What happened?"

Elise felt the color rush back to her face. "Of course. We only made it back a little over a hundred years before the malfunction. We were able to bring the capsule back intact." Elise wanted to tell him about Captain Garrett, but now was not the time, not with a room full of press people.

"I'll get back to you." It sounded more like a threat than a promise.

Elise ended the call. The evening T.V. and newfeeds would carry the story of her failure. She knew that the press would soon converge on her office to get her story, and they had to move Captain Garrett before then. She rose to go back into the lab. Entering the anteroom, she noticed that the lights were off. She clicked them on and gasped. Captain Garrett was gone!

"Richard!" Elise yelled, panic choking her voice.

Richard and Wende rushed into the room.

"Where is the captain?" Elise demanded.

Richard was flustered. "I just checked! He was right here!"

"Wende, start checking all the rooms on this floor. Richard, come with me. He can't have gotten too far." Elise knew that they had to find him before he got outside the building.

"Elise," Richard called, "he's got his pistol!"

"All right. Be careful. I don't think he's dangerous, but he is frightened. We're going downstairs and work our way up. Let's go."

Elise and Richard ran to the elevator. "If he's going down," she said, "he'll be going down the stairs. It's all he knows."

When Chris awoke, he felt nauseated. He opened his eyes and was surprised to find that he was still in the strange room, although he was alone. He sat up unsteadily. Another wave of nausea swept over him, but he forced it down. He staggered over to the sink and turned the faucet as he had seen Richard do. Water gushed out, startling him. Even more startling was the fact that the water quickly turned hot. Very hot. He splashed some on his face. The only way to clear up this mystery was to get outside, find familiar surroundings and a familiar face.

He found his pistol still in the holster and sword hanging on a nearby chair, but before he had time to strap them on, he heard footsteps approaching. He stuffed the pistol in his pants waist and quickly moved to the door. Cautiously, he opened it. It led to a hallway. He again imitated Richard and clicked off the overhead light (amazing thing), and slipped into the hall, closing the door behind himself.

Several feet down the hall, he came to a set of double narrow doors, but they had no handles. There was a sign above the doors with the word – Elevator. It meant nothing to him. He looked down the hall to his left. There, at the end of the hall was a sign he recognized - Stairway. He ran down the hall and pulled open the heavy door. At least he now knew that whatever building he was in, he wasn't on the ground floor. He must be one, possibly two floors up. What amazed him was the fact that he had never seen a two-story building in the Montana Territory.

He started down the stairs. By the time he had gone down five flights, he knew something was wrong. He had never gone down so many steps before in his life. His boots didn't make it any easier walking, and his heavy uniform was making it unbearably hot... just like the Montana Territory. Undeterred, he kept going.

By the twentieth floor, he felt as if he must be in the very bowels of the earth. He had to stop and rest every couple of flights now. He took out his bandana and wiped the perspiration that flowed across his face and neck. It's can't be much farther, he told himself. He had come so far already. Twenty floors later, he reached ground level.

Gasping for breath, Chris staggered out into the lobby. Leaning against a smooth granite wall for a moment to catch his breath, he closed his eyes to shut the light from his pounding head.

"Captain Garrett, are you all right?"

Chris stood straight up but refused to open his eyes. That voice! He was having that crazy daydream again.

"Captain, please come back upstairs with us."

It couldn't be. He was certain no one had followed him down the stairs.

"Captain…"

Chris swallowed. He was going to open his eyes and he was going to see the grassy slopes of the Montana Territory. Slowly, he raised his eyelids.

"Captain, are you all right?"

"You!" he shouted. It wasn't possible. The woman doctor had followed him, and she wasn't even breathing hard. What manner of place was this?

"Please come with me," Elise said softly, trying to convince him to listen to her. "Let us explain. At least give us a chance."

Chris was in no mood for jawing explanations. He was one frightened soldier. He made a quick decision and bolted between Elise and Richard, knocking her to the floor. He saw light streaming in from the large glass doors that led outside and made a beeline for it. He felt trapped inside.

"Don't lose him!" Elise shouted.

Richard hesitated, helped Elise to her feet, then galloped after the disappearing Captain. "He won't go far once he's outside," he shouted.

As Chris reached the door and reached for the handle, the door whooshed open in front of him. What the…? He didn't wait to see who had opened it, but raced outside, and was completely staggered by what greeted him. The few people on the sidewalk hardly paid him any attention, nor he them, but the gigantic high-rise buildings that blocked his view and the strange large objects, some lining the sidewalk and others moving noisily up and down the street with no visible means of horsepower, frightened him.

Strange, loud noises battered his ears, and the thick, hard to breathe air attacked his eyes and lungs. He turned to his right and ran. At the first corner, he turned right again. The next street was crowded with people and the wagon/contraptions moving in spurts; quick take-offs and stops. People threaded their way across the street with apparent unconcern for the strange moving machines.

Terrified, he paused but for a moment before charging headlong into the traffic. Tires squealed, horns blared, and voices screamed. A car brushed into him, knocking him down. He lay stunned. The car stopped and the driver leaped out, shouting at Chris as he moved. "You clown! What're you doing out in the middle of the street?"

He never finished his tirade. Chris drew his pistol and fired at the terrifying machine that had run him down. The driver turned and dived behind another car. There were more shouts and screams. Everything was in confusion.

Chris struggled to his feet and limped on across the street. His leg hurt painfully, but he didn't think it was broken. He stopped to take stock of the situation in the street. People were doing either one of two things; running for cover from the shooting, or else standing by calmly, staring at the maniac in dressed in the funny costume. Chris didn't take any time to gauge public reactions. He wanted to see what the machines were doing. He limped on down the sidewalk and turned up a deserted alley.

Richard ran out of the building in time to see the captain turn the corner and head towards the busiest part of town. He groaned and ran after him, reaching the busy street just as the shooting occurred. There was nothing to hide behind, so he hugged the nearest wall. By the time he uncovered his head, Elise was standing by his side, and Captain Garrett was nowhere in sight. They ran to the street together. Traffic was already moving again, and people were resuming their way along the sidewalk.

They scanned both sides of the street for the unmistakable blue uniform. Nothing. They dashed across the street through traffic. Horns honked angrily at them. Richard ran up to two well dressed, but obviously startled, men.

"Which way did he go?" Richard shouted.

The shorter of the two turned to his partner. "Is he addressin' us, James?" He spoke with a Brooklyn accent.

"Please, did you see him?" Richard asked impatiently. "He must have come right by here."

The one called James held his gold handled cane up in front of him. He wore white gloves. "See whom?" he asked politely.

"The captain… the army officer! Which way did he go?"

James stared at Richard. Gregory, the shorter gentleman, walked around Richard, looking him over, then stopped right behind him.

Richard could see that he wasn't getting anywhere. He changed his tactics. "The nut in the blue uniform," he shouted, "which way?"

James pulled back and put a white glove to his ear. "There is absolutely no reason to shout at me, sir. My hearing is quite fine, thank you."

Elise ran up and tugged at Richard's sleeve. "We're wasting time," she said impatiently.

James looked her over with appreciation. "Are you with him?" He pointed at Richard.

Elise nodded, but hardly looked at James. She was still scanning the street. "Yes."

"And why are you looking for this other chap? Is he in some sort of trouble?"

Gregory circled Elise as he had Richard, brushing against

her a couple of times. Elise hardly noticed. But she was quickly losing her patience. This encounter was using up time. They had only spent perhaps one minute or so talking, but that amount of time could prove fatal to the captain. "No, he's not in trouble, but we need very badly to catch up with him." Not in trouble yet, she thought.

James and Gregory had indeed seen the character in the blue uniform. He had made such a spectacular appearance on the street that it was hard to miss him. James raised a gloved hand and pointed in the direction Chris had taken. "I believe he went that way... and he seemed to be in quite a hurry. He isn't a fugitive from the law, is he?" A shocked look crossed his face.

"Come on!" Richard shouted without answering James' last query. He grabbed Elise's arm and dragged her along behind him.

Elise shouted, "Thanks!" without looking back. She shook loose from Richard, got her balance, then ran close on his heels.

Gregory stared after them and shook his head. "What do you think of that?"

James wagged his finger. "It takes all kinds, Gregory, never forget that. I'm a great student of perception and I believe that those two are among the crackpots of society." He straightened his tie.

"Do you really think they're crazy?" Gregory asked wide-eyed.

James nodded solemnly. "Look at the way they were dressed. What were those white coats? Did you look closely in the man's eyes? Sheer panic. And the woman, fear."

Gregory shook his head back and forth slowly. "That's amazing, James. I guess you're right, though, it takes all kinds."

"Of course, it does. Now, what did you get?"

Gregory held up his hands. "Nothing much. Wallet, watch, and some keys. The broad didn't have anything."

"A shame but expected. Oh, well, better luck next time."

Richard and Elise ran up the street to the end of the block. Captain Garrett was nowhere in sight. How could that be? It wasn't as if the captain knew where he was going. Elise turned to a young couple leaning against the corner building. "Please, did you see an Army Captain run down here just a minute ago?"

They just looked at her.

Richard stopped some people walking by, asking about the captain, but they just stared, as if angry about being accosted by a stranger, and then they went on their way.

The street had returned to its normal everyday state as if the past few minutes of commotion had never happened.

"Maybe those guys were wrong," Richard finally said.

Elise put a hand on Richard's shoulder for support and shook a pebble out of her shoe. "How could they be wrong?" she asked wearily. "It would be pretty hard to confuse the captain with anybody else." She was really worried now. Every passing minute only increased the odds of something happening to the confused and frightened Captain.

She wanted to run in every direction at once. She wanted to shake people around her and ask why they wouldn't help. She wanted to cry.

Richard was mumbling to himself. Somebody on the street besides the two who had directed them must have seen the captain. Somebody had to have noticed him shooting at whatever it was he had shot at... whatever he shot at! What had he shot at? His eyes widened. What if the captain hadn't shot at anything. What if someone had shot him, loaded him in a car and... who would kidnap an army officer fresh from the past? Who even knew he was fresh from the past? He walked over to the nearest doorway and peered inside the store. "You know," he said, "it's really odd."

"What is?" Elise asked.

"The way Captain Garrett came into this world... he just appeared. And now..."

Indeed, it seemed that Captain Garrett had disappeared just as suddenly.

Richard looked at Elise. "Now what?"

But Elise was already moving, searching.

CHAPTER 4

Elise and Richard searched the entire street, checking in every store, every doorway and every alley for two blocks either way. Captain Garrett just wasn't to be found.

Richard was disgusted as he leaned against the entry way to a small mom and pop grocery store. "There are so many kooks running around loose these days, and so many shootings, nobody even notices another one."

Elise stopped to catch her breath. The heavy smog just wasn't as refreshing as real air used to be. She looked at Richard. He was panting, too. She looked at him again. He was wearing his white lab coat, and his hair was blown wildly from running. Elise started to laugh.

"Whatever is so funny?" Richard asked with a sidelong glance.

"You're talking about running around loose," she laughed. "Look at us!"

Richard turned to look closely at her. She was wearing her lab coat, and her hair was tangled every which way from running, too. He had to chuckle as he thought of what a picture the pair of them must make. She looked like the mad scientist. He must look worse.

"Okay, okay," he said, "let's stop and think. If you were suddenly plucked up from the past and thrust into this city with no warning, where would you go?"

"That's ridiculous," Elise chided him. "How do I know where I'd go? Captain Garrett is obviously terrified, and probably in a state of shock."

"You don't suppose the molecular acceleration process could be self-reversing, do you? I mean, could we be searching for a man who is no longer here?"

Elise shook her head. "I've thought of that, too, but I doubt it's happened. The acceleration needs an outside stimulus to get it going. Almost any kind of energy can keep it going once it's started, though. I've read some recent papers that suggest emotional energy may even be enough to continue the process, and I'm certain that the captain is in enough of an emotionally charged state for that, but it still takes some kind of initial resonant energy."

"How about if he were to receive an electrical shock of some kind? I mean, suppose he stuck his finger in an electrical outlet to see what it was, or something. Would that do it?"

"I don't know, Richard. You're asking things that haven't been explored yet for obvious reasons. We've never had a person as part of the project to experiment on before. We don't have any idea what the time process has done to his system, or his mind. All I can say is that I doubt it has reversed itself. He's got to be around here somewhere."

"If he's hiding anywhere close, he's doing an amazing job. He's obviously run off. The big question is, where? And why? Why did he run from us? We were going to help him."

Elise rubbed her eyes. "Running away is a normal human reaction. We're all afraid of the things we don't understand." She paused, thinking.

Richard watched the frown on her face.

"A normal human reaction... Richard, if he's reacting naturally, what would he do?"

"I already asked you first."

"He's probably looking for some kind of familiar ground so he can get his bearings."

Richard scoffed. "I'm afraid there's not much familiarity between these wretched streets and the Montana Territory."

Elise's eyes suddenly lit up. "How about the park? Carnegie Park is only a couple of blocks from here. It's got grass, trees..."

Richard looked at her disappointed. "Elise, how could Captain Garrett possibly know that?"

She frowned again. "You're right. What do we do next?" She slumped against the wall next to Richard.

Richard thought for a moment. "First thing is, you had better call Wende and tell her what the heck is going on. She's probably worried to death. Then we keep searching every street and alley until we find him. He's bound to turn up someplace. He's *got* to turn up someplace!"

Elise felt her pockets. "I don't have my pocket tel. It's at the office."

Richard didn't have his tel either. His was also at the office on his desk. " We'll have to borrow one someplace."

A store clerk finally agreed to let them use his tel, but kept a beady eye on them, ready to take chase if they took off with it.

Elise saw Richard suddenly start dancing around. "What are you doing?"

Richard reached into his pants pocket. A concerned look crossed his face. Something was wrong. His hands went to his other pockets in turn.

Elise waited. "What's the matter?"

Richard glanced at her. "I've lost my keycards someplace... and my wallet... and my watch!" He frantically searched each of his pockets again. "All I've got left is a couple of dollars in change. I've been ripped off!"

"By whom?"

"I don't know. Probably by one of those weirdos in the street."

"Maybe they'll turn up," Elise said doubtfully. "I can give you the spare house key you left with me. On a hunch, she dialed the Wende's pocket tel number.

Richard pursed his lips afraid to tell Elise that it wasn't his house keys that were missing… it was his set of keys to General Amalgamated Lab. He decided to not mention that fact just yet, although a shiver ran up his spine.

Wende answered Elise's call on the second ring. "Wende, this is Elise."

"Oh, doctor, yes… hello."

Elise was puzzled. Wende's voice sounded strange.

"Wende, is something wrong?"

Thre was a strangled laugh. "Oh, things are a bit hectic here right now, you know. We're just a little busy with everyone here."

Elise thought for a minute. Everyone here…? "The press! Are the news people there, Wende?" Suddenly she was glad she hadn't called the lab number.

Wende laughed again. "Very perceptive." Her voice lowered. "Where are you? Everyone is asking for you."

Richard tugged at Elise's sleeve. "What's the matter?"

She covered the receiver. "Press. Wende can't talk." She spoke back into the tel. "Wende, listen… our friend is somewhere out in the streets. We've lost him for the time being."

"In those clothes?" Wende asked quietly.

"I know it doesn't sound possible, but he's gone. It's simply amazing what people don't notice these days. Can you stall the press?"

"No." It was a bold statement.

"You've got to."

Wende sighed. "All right. If you insist. I'd love to…"

"I'm sorry," Elise said tight lipped. "I'm surprised that Doctor Bruce even let them in the lab."

"Weren't we all."

"We've got to find… our friend. Tell the press that I'm upstairs checking programs or something. Tell them anything but the truth."

"It's not nice to fool Mother Nature," Wende said.

Now it was Elise's turn to sigh. "I know. As soon as we locate him, we'll stash him someplace safe, and I'll come let you off the hook. Okay?"

"That would be peachy. And thanks for calling. It's been a real pleasure hearing from you."

Elise gave the tel back to the relieved clerk with a thanks. "I think it will be better if we stick together," she said grimly to Richard.

Richard had no intentions of leaving her alone. "Right," was all he said.

Captain Garrett stopped in an alcove off the alley to catch his breath. The pain in his leg was less intense, but never-the-less a hindrance. The woman doctor had been right. He wasn't anywhere near prepared for what was outside that building. There was just no describing the terrifying... what? - train-like machine? - that had attacked him. He felt certain that he had disabled one of them – the one that had hit him.

The air was filled with a thousand terrible noises and smells. It was difficult to breathe. The thick and heavy odors were making him nauseous again. He looked up at the sky, framed in by tall buildings on every side. Taller buildings than anything he had ever seen in his life. The sky was a yellowish-gray color instead of the bright, clear blue that he was used to. The sun was blocked by the buildings, and the pall diffused the light so that he couldn't even locate its approximate position. He fought back a sensation he was unfamiliar with even in all the campaigns he had been involved in while in the army....a helpless feeling of panic.

The kinds and intensity of the noises that assaulted his ears defied description. The thunder of a buffalo stampede. The screams, whistles and rattles of a railroad train. Voices, horns... all this and more in a frightening cacophony.

His head pounded and he felt on the verge of passing out as he gaped open-mouthed at the jet screaming overhead, leaving a trail of vapor in its wake. What manner of creature...

or could it possibly be a machine? In the air? He forced himself to get up and stumble down the alley. He had never seen streets so compacted as these. Perhaps they were cobblestone worn down smooth. The buildings reached so high upward that it made him dizzy to stare up at them... and whatever town this was, something mighty important must be going on for so many people to congregate all in one place. The rest of the territory must be deserted.

He looked cautiously up and down the next street before venturing forth. It looked as unnerving as the last street. He watched, fascinated by the strange machines moving in the streets. There were people sitting in them. Now that he was more settled down, he could see that they were some sort of horseless carriages... maybe steam powered like a locomotive... although there was no smoke or steam billowing from them like a train. He felt slightly foolish now for having shot at one. He closed his eyes. Now what?

Could the woman doctor possibly be right? Was this indeed the future? How did he get here? One minute he was standing in the wide and open expanse of the Montana Territory, the next minute someplace crowded, noisy, and mostly made of stone. Maybe he had been a little hasty running away from the doctor. It was unimaginable, but it was also hard to dispute the facts of what he was observing. If only his head would clear, then he could sort it all out, get his bearings. There was too much to take in, though, and so he limped down the sidewalk. He noticed how oddly everyone was dressed, and he was conscious of a few people staring at him, commenting and laughing. Most shocking were the women and how they were dressed in public! Where were their dresses? It seemed that they all wore men's trousers.

In order to get away from the stares, he stepped into a nearby doorway. The strong smell of food wrapped around him in a cloud. Suddenly, he was shoved farther inside as a group of young people shouldered their way in past him. He quickly reached for his pistol but held off when he saw that the people were ignoring him. They had pressed to the counter and were ordering food. What manner of place was this? He watched as the man behind the counter prepared their order. A long strip of meat laid in a long piece of bread, and squirted with a glop of yellow, syrupy material. Not very appetizing looking.

"Next."

Chris looked at the man.

"Whatdoyouwant?"

Chris stared at him. "I beg your pardon?"

"Whatdoyouwantahotdog?"

Chris knew it was a question, and he could decipher the words 'hot' and 'dog'. Hot dog? Indians ate dog meat sometimes, but not white men. Not unless they were starving. Is this what the future had come to, a race of starving people?

The man stared at him. "Either order, or move along, General."

Chris looked up sharply. General? The man just stared at him impatiently. "Dog," Chris mumbled.

He watched as the man took what appeared to be a limp cigar shaped object and slapped it into a piece of bread shaped the same way. "No yellow stuff," Chris said. Whatever it was, it didn't look very good.

The man handed over the hot dog and Chris took a hesitating bite. He had never tasted dog meat before, and while the thought wasn't very pleasant, it actually didn't taste bad. Very salty. But then, he hadn't eaten anything since this morning, or was it yesterday?

The man then held out his hand and said, "That'llbeabuck."

Chris looked blankly at him. "What?"

The man looked angry. "What's a matter? You deaf? That'll be a buck," he shouted more or less clearly.

A buck? Chris was puzzled. Obviously, the man was trading deer meat for dog meat. Not a bad deal if you could pull it off, but Chris had no deer meat. In fact, he had nothing with which to barter.

"I don't have any deer meat," he told him.

The man screwed up his face. "What're you talking, about? Are ya gonna pay for that dog, or do I callacop?"

Callacop? It sounded like something to drink.

The man reached across the counter and grabbed Chris by the collar. "Now, lookahere, General Custer. You pay for that dog or I'm gonna beat it out of ya. Do you understand that, wise guy?"

In one smooth, quick action, Chris brought his pistol up and punched it in the man's fat belly. His eyes widened as he looked down at the gun.

"Okay, okay... take it easy! Take the hot dog. I don't know nothin', okay? No hard feelin's." He dropped Chris like a hot rock and pressed himself back against the wall.

Chris backed out of the store, stuck the pistol back in his pants, and ran down the street, stuffing the hot dog in his mouth. He had a couple of near misses with the noisy horseless carriages when crossing the streets, but no one seemed to be chasing him. Then he came to a grassy area with trees. He ran to it.

There were very few people in the park. Chris had seen parks before in the East, in some of the big cities, but few were as lush and green as this one appeared to be. It was definitely quieter and cooler here. Chris sat on a nearby bench to rest and think. This was his first real chance to take stock of the situation. First: he was definitely not in the Montana Territory any longer. Second: whatever city this was, he had never been here before. Third: the woman doctor and her story of the future... could it be true? There were many things that had happened that he couldn't explain any other way. He sure was someplace, and it might as well be in the future. Trying to imagine being taken into the future only made his head pound worse.

"Heyya, buddy!"

Chris spun around, fell to his knee with his pistol in his hand, ready for anything.

"Don't shoot!" the drunk cried. "Don't shoot! I gotta wife

and kids... someplace."

Chris stared at the grubby figure. He looked like Chris felt. Slowly, he lowered the pistol.

The drunk was crying now. "Don't shoot, please, don't shoot. All I wanted was a few cents for a crummy meal, but you keep it. I don't want it. Don't shoot!"

Chris studied the pathetic figure crumpling to the ground before him, great sobs racking his thin body. "What year is this?" Chris demanded.

The drunk looked carefully at Chris, studying his face, then his dirty uniform. Chris' hat was pulled to one side, like a side show comic. The drunk started to laugh, rolling back on his knees.

"What's so funny?"

The drunk was almost hysterical. "You," he choked. "I thought you was gonna mug me, but look at you..." He had to stop talking to catch his breath for a fresh burst of laughter. "You're drunker 'n I am!" With this pronouncement, he unceremoniously fell to the ground convulsing with drunken mirth.

Chris' eyes hardened, then he stood up, putting his gun back in his pants, and slowly walked away.

The sun had settled down behind the immense buildings by now, and the smog filled sky was filtering out any remaining light. As Chris limped down the path, he was suddenly startled by the streetlights abruptly snapping on. He cautiously limped over to one of the light poles. Gingerly, he reached out and touched the aluminum post. "Gas lights that light themselves. Wagons that move by themselves..." His head began to spin. He had to sit down.

There was another bench twenty yards ahead. Shaking his head, trying to clear it, he hobbled towards the bench. He suddenly realized that what he really needed was sleep, anything to make his head stop hurting. He was almost upon the bench before he saw that someone was sitting there already. He squinted to focus his eyes and saw that the occupant was an elderly lady. She cast furtive sidelong glances at Chris as he limped up and sat down. Another encounter, he thought as he rubbed his eyes with the back of his calloused hands.

"Are you all right?"

Chris wasn't sure how to answer. He understood the question well enough, but he wasn't sure if he was all right or not. He was inclined to think not.

"Young man, I asked if you were all right."

Chris looked at her. She was staring at his filthy uniform. "Yes, I'm sorry. I'm all right… I think."

"Drunk," she sniffed.

He laid his head back against the bench. She was the second one to accuse him of being drunk. "No ma'am, I'm not drunk."

"Sick?"

Chris didn't answer.

"Crazy," she decided.

"That I may be," he agreed. "What year is this?"

The old lady stared at him. "What kind of a silly question is that?" she asked.

"Please, I've got to know. What year is it?" His voice was stronger.

"It's twenty-forty-five."

"Say it again."

She hesitated. "It's… two thousand and forty-five."

Chris' eyes widened. "It can't be! You're lying!" He looked like a wild man; disheveled, dirty, scared, and dressed in his uniform, he scared the old lady. "You're lying!" he shouted. His head throbbed unbearably.

The old lady started to get up. Chris stretched out his arms to pull her back down. "Tell me you're lying!" he screamed.

Chris wasn't aware of the old lady's quick movement, but he felt the exploding pain when she clobbered him over the head with her oversized purse. He fell to his knees and was faintly aware of her screaming as she clubbed him again. "Help! Help! Police! Help! Help!"

When she hit him for the third time, he slumped to the ground in a welcome state of unconsciousness.

Richard and Elise were having a great deal of trouble following the captain's trail. It was simply amazing how nobody noticed a strange acting character in an old blue army uniform.

"You would think they see this kind of thing every day," Richard complained. "Come to think about it," he said as they passed a person of indeterminable sex, dressed in a wildly colored poncho... and possibly nothing else... "maybe he's not so out of place after all. I guess he's no weirder than the other freaks in this city."

About halfway down the block, they passed a small hot dog shop. The dubious smells from within reminded Elise that they hadn't eaten all day, and it was now getting dark. "Let's grab a bite," she urged.

They entered the greasy looking diner. Richard ordered two hot dogs and coffee. They watched as the corpulent figure behind the counter prepared their order.

"Well, he couldn't just disappear," Richard said. "Somebody is bound to notice him sooner or later."

"We could spend all night looking for him," Elise sighed. "Maybe we're just going to have to call for help."

"Call for help. That's a brilliant idea," Richard scoffed forgetting he was talking to his immediate supervisor. "Who do we call? And what do we tell them? That we're looking for a United States Cavalry officer?"

"Hey."

They turned to the vendor. He was staring at their white lab coats.

"You two lookin' for a nut in a blue uniform?"

Richard's pulse quickened. "Yes, a man dressed in an older looking blue army uniform. Have you seen him?"

"Sure, I seen 'em."

"When?"

"Must be an hour ago or more. He held me up."

Elise sucked in her breath. "Held you up?"

"Yeah, he took a hot dog."

Richard stared at the vendor. "A hot dog?" The vendor nodded. "That's all? A hot dog?"

"Yeah. He was a real nut; you know what I mean? Instead of payin', he mumbled somethin' real spacey about tradin' or somethin', and then he pulls this pistol. It was a real old lookin' thing and I didn't know if it would work or not, but I was afraid that if he tried to shoot it, it might blow up and hurt both of us. So, I let him have the dog."

"Did you call the police?" Elise asked.

"Over a hot dog? Please, lady, business isn't exactly terrific, but do I look like one crummy hot dog might close me? Maybe you could pay for it, huh?" He belched loudly and rubbed his fat belly.

Richard was excited to get back on Chris' trail. "Which way did he go?"

"Well, he backed out of here and took off like a shot up that-a-way," he pointed with one of the hot dogs.

Elise and Richard raced for the door.

"Hey," shouted the surprised vendor, "how about these dogs?"

Richard stopped and reached deep into a pocket. He extracted the last of his change and tossed it on the counter. "Keep the change!" he called as he ran out the door. When he caught up to Elise, she expressed what he had already figured out. "The park! Don't ask me how, but he's headed for the park!"

They ran, dodging traffic as they crossed against red lights to get quickly to the park. They reached the edge of the grass and Elise grabbed Richard by the arm. "Let's split up. We can cover more area that way."

"Not a chance," Richard argued. "You don't know what kind of nuts you might meet in a place like this after dark. Muggers...and... muggers..." his voice trailed off.

Elise cast him a loving look. "You're worried about me."

"I'm worried about me. Let's go."

Together they walked down the path, afraid to poke in the dark places. The streetlights cast a dull glow, causing frightening shadows, like people crouching in waiting.

"Captain? Captain, where are you?" Richard called. "Captain, it's me, Richard and Doctor McAllister."

"Heyya, buddy!"

Elise screamed and Richard hugged her. "Oh, God! A mugger!" Richard had heard all the terrible stories about this park.

"Ya got three bucks for a cup of coffee?"

Richard opened his eyes and stared at the shabbily dressed figure before them. "Where did you come from?" he said, shakily.

"Oh, I was right over there," the man said in a raspy voice. "Got any spare change?"

Elise, over her initial fright, asked, "Have you been here very long?"

The man looked her over. "Eight years," he said, picking his teeth with a broken toothpick.

"No, no. I mean, very long tonight. Have you been right here for, say, the last couple of hours?"

The man narrowed his eyes and shifted his weight. "Sure, I been here. Why?" He eyed them suspiciously.

"Did you see a man, fairly tall, medium build, dark hair, wearing a hat... good looking..." Elise broke off as the man began laughing.

"Lady, that describes half the guys in Kelly's Liquor Store this minute." He chuckled. "I did see one odd bird here today, though. Some nut dressed up like General Custer. A real whacko. They shouldn't let people like that loose on the street. It's all them budget cuts, ya know." He began to guffaw. "I thought he was a mugger."

Richard and Elise exclaimed together, "That's him!"

"Where is he?" Elise asked excitedly.

The man slowly took a broken comb from his torn pocket

and ran it through his sparse hair. "He's not here."

"For God's sake, man, we can see that!" Richard shouted. "Where did he go?"

The man straightened up, affronted, and put his comb back in his pocket. "There's no need to shout at me," he said. "I haven't done anything to you. Just because I'm a little down on my luck presently, and I'm hard pressed for meals, that don't give you no right to yell at me."

Richard closed his eyes and counted to ten. "I'm sorry."

"Please," Elise interrupted, "we're looking to help the man we're looking for. He's... sick."

"Uh huh. Yep, I figgered you guys was from the nut house by the way your dressed an' all."

Richard's patience was drawing thin. "Where is he?"

The man looked Richard over carefully, then turned to Elise. "I don't think I like him," he confided.

Elise reluctantly, and out of sheer desperation, put her arm around the man's shoulder. "He means well. He's just worried about our... patient. Please, which way did he go?"

"Well," the man sniffed, "I reckon he's locked up by now."

Elise almost choked. "Locked up? What do you mean?"

"Right after I left him, he attacked old Betty. I saw the whole thing."

"What!" Elise cried.

The man laughed. "Actually, nobody in his right mind would try to attack old Betty. She's mean. And she hits. Sometimes she bites. Happens every time somebody sits on her bench."

"So, what happened," Elise asked fearfully.

"The cops came and took him away." He casually inspected his dirty fingernails. "Don't happen very often. Usually, there's not a cop to be seen when you want one, but this time they was cruisin' by right when she started yellin'." He brushed a cloud of dust from his sleeve.

Elise turned to Richard; her eyes filled with fear.

"Do you know where they took him?" Richard asked.

"I ought to know well enough," the man laughed. "I've spent enough nights there myself. Two down and two over."

Richard grabbed Elise's hand and pulled her away. "Let's go!" They ran off together.

"Hey," the man called, "how 'bout some change? I'm homeless, you know! Name's Jeffy, in case there's a reward or anything." He watched them disappear, then stumbled on his way.

"Yep, he's here all right," the night sergeant affirmed. "We got him locked up in the drunk tank. Tried to attack some old lady over in the park. You never know about these weirdos. Sometimes they're harmless, sometimes they're not. We haven't even booked him yet. The old lady didn't even come in to file a complaint. He was out like a light when they brought him in, so we put him in the tank 'till he sobers up."

Elise was relieved to hear that the captain hadn't been booked yet. She was afraid that if the police tried to identify Captain Garrett, they would find out that he doesn't really exist... or at least isn't supposed to exist... yet. It would be a mess.

"Hey," the sergeant looked them over carefully," are you guys from General?"

Elise looked alarmed. "General?" How could he know they worked at General Amalgamated?

"Yeah, General Hospital. You guys after this guy?"

Richard stepped forward. "Yes, yes, that's it. I'm Doctor... um... Smith, and this is Nurse... um...I don't know... she's my nurse."

The sergeant nodded. "Uh huh. Then you *are* from General."

"Yes, and the captain... I mean the man you are holding... managed to escape from his unit this afternoon. We trailed him to the park, but we lost him. Then we found him here, and now we would like to take custody of him, if you don't mind."

"He's nuts, huh?" the sergeant asked wide-eyed. Richard

nodded solemnly. "You know," the sergeant whispered, "when he was brought in, I thought to myself then that there was something didn't seem right about the poor guy. I mean, did you notice the way he's dressed, and all? I mean the blue uniform. And he had a pistol, a real antique. I don't know that it would still work, although it was loaded."

Richard shook his head. "Yes, Mr. ... um... Smith..." He winced as he made up the name. Elise winced, too.

"Smith? Didn't you say your name Smith?"

Richard squeaked out a laugh. "Yes, isn't that a funny coincidence? Anyway, Mr. Smith thinks he is General Custer. The gun is completely harmless, of course. As part of his cure, we let him act out his fantasy. So, sergeant..."

"Guffy."

"Sergeant Guffy, if you would be kind enough to turn Cap... I mean, Mr. Smith loose, we will take him back to the hospital, and off your hands." He smiled at the sergeant.

The sergeant grabbed a set of keys from his desk drawer and stood up. "Sure, Doc. Gee, I didn't realize he was so sick, or I wouldn't have locked him up in the drunk tank. We got a padded cell for nuts. You don't suppose he might have hurt himself, do you?"

"No," Richard smiled. "He is quite harmless, actually." He held the door for Elise. "Nurse?"

Elise smiled, too, and shook her head. "Thank you... Doctor."

They clanged through several heavy metal doors before reaching the cell-lined hallway. Raucous laughter could be heard from a far end cell.

"That's the drunk tank," the sergeant sniffed. Elise and Richard hurried down the hall. Captain Garrett stood against one wall, hands on hips, facing several drunks. They were all laughing and pointing at the captain. One of them called out, "Then what happened, General" and the whole group fell on one another laughing.

Elise called to Chris. "Captain, it's Doctor McAllister. Are you all right?"

The sergeant turned to Richard. "I thought you said she was a nurse."

Richard shushed him. "Don't let on. Mr. Smith thinks she's a doctor."

Sergeant Guffy nodded confidingly.

Chris spun around at the sound of a familiar voice. Relief flooded his face. "I didn't think I'd ever say this, but am I glad to see you!"

One of the drunks hollered. "Aw, yer not gonna take him away, are ya? We was just getting' acquainted."

Sergeant Guffy unlocked the cell and opened the door into the hall. "Get back, boys. Let the man through."

Chris quickly made his way across the cell and stepped out between Elise and Richard. "Get me out of here," he said anxiously. "Take me anywhere and tell me anything but get me out of here!"

Sergeant Guffy leaned over to Richard and whispered, "You gonna put him in a strait jacket or anything, Doc?"

Richard smiled. "No, he'll be all right. Could I please have the pistol back, also?"

The sergeant nodded eagerly. "Sure, Doc, sure. I got it up front. You can get it on the way out. There are just a couple of papers for you to sign, too."

Richard paused. Papers? That could be bad. He put his arm around the sergeant and steered him away from the others. "Sergeant, you said that Mr. Smith hadn't been booked yet, right? Then I need a little favor. Mr. Smith belongs to a prominent family here in the city, you'd know the name, but, of course, I can't say the name due to confidentiality laws. Anyway, it would be very embarrassing to the family if this little incident got out. What are the chances we could keep this on the quiet? You know, no names or papers, or fingerprints... anything like that."

"Sure, sure, Doc. I get ya," the sergeant nodded knowingly.

They hurried to the front desk, collected the pistol, and

hustled the captain out of the door of the police station.

Elise exploded. "You idiot! Do you realize what you almost caused?"

Chris was taken by surprise. "What I almost caused? Wait a minute. I didn't ask to be brought here... wherever here is."

Richard put a stop to the imminent fight. "Look," he said, "we are all tired. A lot has happened in the last few hours, especially to you, Captain. We can't stand here in the middle of the street all night, and we can't take Captain Garrett back to the lab. What are we going to do?"

Elise turned on Richard. "How about we just take him back to the hospital, Doctor?" she asked sarcastically.

"Elise..."

"Okay, okay," Elise apologized. "You're right, we can't take him back to the lab." She thought for a moment. "We'll have to take him to my apartment for the time being."

"Your apartment?"

"You have any better ideas?"

"You could send me back," Chris offered.

"I'll stay with you," Richard decided.

"I don't think that will be necessary," Elise said. "I'm pretty sure that the captain will behave himself now. Won't you, Captain?"

"Meek as a lamb, Ma'am," he smiled weakly.

Richard still had doubts in his mind. "Elise, we still don't know the aftereffects of time travel. This man needs to be placed under study, not invited to your apartment as an overnight guest.

"*If* there are any aftereffects," Elise argued. "So far, Captain Garrett's reactions have been those which we might normally expect in a situation like his. Nothing more, nothing less."

"I'm staying," Richard declared flatly as he stepped to the curb to hail a taxi.

Elise kept an eye on Chris. He was staring at the marvelous display of neon signs and lights. It was a dazzling display of color and light to eyes whose brightest sight up to now had been the soul stirring display of bright, twinkling stars in a crisp, clear Montana Territory night sky; something Elise and Richard had never experienced.

Elise was touched as Chris' eyes swelled to take in all that was offered to him. She tried to put herself in his place. It was beyond any possible reasoning. Suddenly she knew that he must be an extraordinary man to bear up under the strain of time travel. She just couldn't fathom suddenly being thrust into an unimaginable future.

Richard whistled, and a cab pulled over to them. Richard opened the back door and held it for Elise and Captain Garrett. Chris had dodged back when the cab pulled over, memories of the afternoon's experience stabbing at his mind. Elise grabbed his hand to reassure him. He gripped her hand tightly.

"It's a taxicab," she told him.

Chris still couldn't believe it. A horseless carriage. "What makes it go?" he asked.

Richard laughed. "It's a long story, Captain. It's run by an internal combustion engine. Most engines are switching to electric now, though, thanks to the Mideast trouble shutting off most petroleum supplies."

Chris was staring blankly at him.

"Just get in," Elise urged. "We've got a lot of explaining to do."

Chris hesitated. He wasn't sure about getting into the carriage... taxicab... whatever. Elise released her hand and got in the cab. Reluctantly, Chris followed her. Richard got in last and shut the door.

The driver turned in his seat, staring at the three of them. Pursing his lips, he asked, "The circus... the theater, or the funny farm?"

Elise and Richard broke out in laughter, and Chris merely sat in his seat in confusion. Richard gave Elise's address as the driver slammed the cab in gear and roared away with a screech of the tires. Chris' eyes widened even farther as they narrowly missed several other cars, the driver swerving and dodging down the street.

Elise took Chris' arm. "You get used to it," she said reassuringly.

Chris nodded slightly, then squeezed his eyes shut, not wanting to see when they crashed. It was worse than a run-away wagon.

Five long minutes later, they pulled up in front of Elise's apartment building. They all got out of the cab, Chris shaking slightly. Elise borrowed some change from the startled doorman and paid the cabby. They watched as he roared off in a cloud of swirling dust.

Chris looked up at the glass-fronted building. One hundred and eight stories. It was one of the taller apartment buildings in the city. Rents started at thirty-eight hundred dollars per month for a single bedroom apartment, but they were comfortable. Chris stood staring, open-mouthed, his eyes following all the way to the top of the building. It was almost fifty times taller than any building he had ever seen before. He stared up until he began to feel dizzy.

"You live clear up there?" he asked Elise.

"Not clear to the top," she assured him. I only live on the ninety-second floor. Mine is apartment 920-B."

Chris was staggered. A veritable house in the clouds. "Nine-twenty? You mean to tell me that there are nine hundred houses up there?"

Elise laughed. "No, there are no houses up there. Only apartments, and there are well over one thousand apartments in the building." She took his arm and led him into the lobby.

Chris' mind flashed back to this morning. "Wait a minute," he balked, "I'm not going to walk up ninety-two sets of steps. I'll never make it. I don't know how you do it."

Elise laughed again. "Didn't you wonder this morning how we beat you to the ground floor?"

Chris tried to remember. He had assumed that she had just followed him down the steps, but hazily he remembered how rested she was compared to his own breathlessness. His eyes suddenly widened. "Don't tell me you can fly?!" He remembered the large object over the streets. Perhaps then, it wasn't a fantastic bird.

Elise pulled him to the elevator and pushed the 'up' button. While they waited for it to appear, Chris surveyed the surroundings. This late at night, there were very few other people present. He wasn't sure what to call this big room, but it was richly carpeted, well-lit and had lots of polished brass. It was fancier than any hotel he could imagine. Again, Elise felt a moment of compassion for this strong man, now lost, but trying his best to comprehend. The elevator doors opened. Richard looked to see who had opened the door, but there was no one in the little room in front of him. Cautiously, he stuck his head part way in and looked around.

"I don't understand," he said. "It's an empty closet."

Elise pushed him in and stepped in herself, allowing the doors to close. Chris looked to see who had closed the doors. Again, there was no one touching the door. Richard pushed the button for floor '92'. Chris grabbed the safety bars and felt his stomach sickeningly plunge as the elevator shot them up ninety-two floors in less than seven seconds. When the doors automatically opened a moment later, Chris jumped out.

"What was that?" he demanded.

"It's called an elevator," Richard told him, stepping out into the plush carpeted hallway.

Chris stopped as he suddenly became aware that he was no longer in the big room he was in seconds ago. He turned around slowly and carefully, surveying the hall. Elise took his arm again and led him to a near-by window. Slowly, she drew back the curtain. Chris quickly stepped back. From ninety-two floors up, the view was stupendous. He cautiously stepped towards the window again and looked down. It took him a moment to realize that the movement far below was the activity on the street he had just been on.

Elise walked down the hall with Richard. Chris followed trying to absorb the day's events. Elise unlocked her apartment door and they stepped into a spacious living room.

Richard immediately spoke to the computer. "ABBI, call Wende on the closed channel. She's probably worried sick by now." He stood off to one side by the tel display unit and waited for the call to go through.

Chris stood in the doorway until Elise took him by the arm and led him into the room. She looked at his filthy uniform and quickly grabbed a blanket from a closet to spread over her soft, light colored sofa before urging Chris to sit. The whole room was decorated in light, soft earth tones. Chris pulled his pistol from his waistband and laid it on the end table, sat down on the sofa and stretched back in the fluffy cushions, relaxing for the first time that day. Elise smiled at him in relief.

"We've got a few more conveniences than you're used to, I'm sure," she said.

Chris smiled back at her. "Every time I think nothing else could surprise me, doggone if you don't go and surprise me some more."

Elise crossed to the kitchen. "Care for something to drink? It'll help soothe the nerves."

Chris' eyes widened. "Well, I'm glad some things haven't changed in a hundred years. Give me a shot of your best."

"It's a hundred and sixty-nine years," she said as she made a blender full of icy protein shake and poured a glass full for all three of them. "Time just flies by when you're having fun." She handed him his glass.

He looked at the glass with a frown. "It appears that drinks have changed over the years, too. This is whiskey?"

Elise smiled. "Not exactly, but it's good for you."

Chris took a sip and wrinkled his nose.

"All checked in," Richard said, after ABBI terminated the call. "Wende's at home. She managed to stall off the press, although she feared for her life for a time. She said once they all left, she worked on systems until about a half an hour ago. She can't find the cause for the malfunction. She thinks we may have to take out the system memory cards and start from scratch. She also encrypted the video feed so no one would see what we have."

Elise bit her lip. Everything had checked out in perfect working order. This news was extremely frustrating. Going over each program and memory card one by one from the ground up was going to be very time consuming. Time consumption meant, as in all business, money, and the grants wouldn't last forever, not to mention the captain.

"She also says you're famous."

"Famous?"

"Social media and television. Wende says she doesn't think we would have gotten this much exposure if we had been successful. ABBI, turn on the news" Elise's ninety-six-inch Plasma D wall T.V. lit up one wall.

Chris watched in amazement as a full color image of a newscaster came into view. Elise saw his wide-eyed expression.

"Television," she told him. "It transmits images and sound digitally via satellites... I'm afraid it's all rather technical to try to explain to you."

They all watched as the newswoman continued her story. "Causes for the apparent malfunction were still undetermined when we last contacted spokesperson Wende Merrill at General Amalgamated Laboratories. It is indeed unfortunate that Doctor Elise McAllister, director of this time travel project, is unavailable for comment, but Ms. Merrill assured us that Dr. McAllister would contact us when further developments were available. We were able to talk briefly with Doctor Marvin Bruce, founder of G. A. Labs. He expressed disappointment in today's malfunction but did not really see it as a failure. Laser-Radiation testing of dust particles found on the time travel vehicle indicated the particles to be over one hundred years old, proving conclusively that the capsule did travel into the past. Time travel has been accomplished! For possible ramifications, we spoke with noted historian, Professor Milton Sanford of Polytec University."

Professor Sanford appeared on the screen as the station

switched to a clip from the professor's office. He turned and squinted into the glaring light on the camera.

"Obviously, the most exciting prospect is to be able to make contact with persons of the past. To be able to talk directly with, say, the Founding Fathers of our country and get their… uh… gut feelings, if you will, about our constitution and its interpretations. It opens up whole new worlds."

Richard asked ABBI to off the set.

"And somebody named Abby can control that thing?" Chris asked wide eyed.

"To a certain extent," Richard said. "The ABBI System can turn it on and off and change channels and the like, but that's all."

Chris stared at the dark screen. "That's all? That's incredible!"

Elise looked at Richard. "Another shake? I made plenty."

"No, thanks. If you're sure you'll be all right for a while, I'd like to go get my car and bring it here."

Elise was touched by Richard's concern. "Really, Richard, there's no reason for you to stay. I'll be fine."

"No, I'll be back before long. I insist. Captain Garrett can sleep on the couch, and I'll sleep on that over-sized chair. Besides, if the press found out where you live and came here in the morning, how would you explain a man being here with you overnight?"

"How would I explain two of you?" Elise laughed. "All right, you win."

"Lock the door behind me," he insisted.

"Richard, I can't lock him in."

Richard gave a last glance at Chris lying on the couch. "I'll be right back," he announced loudly.

Elise closed the door behind him with a chuckle. She crossed back to the chair across from the couch and sat wearily.

"Richard owns a taxicab, too?" he asked.

Elise was amused. "No, he owns a car."

"What's a car?"

"A car is... well, a taxi is a car..." she stopped, not sure how to explain.

Chris was aware of her predicament. He probably wouldn't understand much of what she told him anyway. There was so much that he didn't understand, so much he wanted to ask. He drank the rest of his protein shake, put a hand to his forehead, then smiled at Elise, tears in his eyes.

"It's cold... gave me a headache."

She smiled. "That's called a brain freeze."

"This is quite an abode," Chris said, looking around. "Things have really changed."

"They call it progress."

"Progress. It's amazing what's done in the name of progress, isn't it? I was in the middle of some progress when I... when I did whatever I did to get here."

Elise sighed. "I'm afraid you didn't do anything to get here."

"How *did* I get here?" he asked.

How could she explain? She wasn't even sure herself. He wasn't supposed to be here. "I'm not sure where to begin."

"Try the beginning."

"It's very technical. I don't think you would understand much of what I'll say."

"Try me."

She looked deep into his questioning eyes, wanting desperately to be able to explain the capsule, the malfunctions, the aborted mission, but how do you explain what you don't understand yourself. Oh, she understood the technical functions of time travel, although admittedly, the reasons for the malfunction were unknown to her as yet, but it was the moral functions that escaped her. It wasn't so much how he got here, as why. The same questions that had bothered her from the beginning now cast their ugly shadows across her mind.

"We were experimenting with a form of time travel." She chose her words carefully. "We are in the initial stages of developing a means to breech a time warp using quantum theory. We believe that phenomena such as superposition and entanglement suggest the possibility of parallel or many universes, many minds, or many histories. By feeding certain data into our computers, and using resonance frequencies, we can accelerate chosen molecules..."

Chris was staring blankly.

Elise smiled. "I told you it was technical."

"Time travel," he mused. "You mean that you have ability to go back to any point in time and bring someone to the future?"

"That certainly would have been an ultimate goal to work towards. But no, this was only the first test. Obviously, it's not perfected yet. You are not part of the plan."

Chris frowned. "What I don't understand is, how did I get here?"

"I don't know."

"I mean, how did I get *here*? This isn't the Montana Territory." His expression widened. "Don't tell me... this isn't the Montana Territory, is it?"

"No, this isn't Montana. We can only theorize, but I believe that time is a vortex, forever spinning outward. The center of the vortex is the present. By sending the time capsule into a time warp, we can control not only time, but to a certain extent, location. When the capsule malfunctioned during our test, apparently it was over the Montana Territory. How it brought you back, we may never know."

"How do I return?"

Elise sipped her shake. She knew this question was coming, but she had hoped not until much later. She looked him right in the eyes. "You can't go back."

Chris' look hardened and he searched her eyes. "What do you mean, I can't go back? I have to go back."

"You can't." Elise looked away momentarily.

"Your machine can't take me?"

"That's part of it." How could she explain that history had run its course and he was branded a deserter for being taken into the future?

"What else?"

Elise sipped her shake again. "You have to understand that the past is now past. It's over and already written in the history books. Events that have happened cannot be redone."

Chris studied her face. "You're saying I can't go back and finish what I was doing?"

Elise closed her eyes. "It's already done."

Chris thought silently for a moment. "You mean that our battle is already over? Of course, it is, if this is more than a hundred years later. Then I've already been through it. Was it a battle? There wasn't supposed to be any fighting, but Colonel Custer thought he had to prove something."

"There was a battle."

"Did we kill many Indians? Poor devils didn't have much of a chance. I led the main column directly into the village. You know, it's really strange to be talking about something I did before I did it... we're really talking about it after I did it, before I did it."

Elise looked away, her eyes suddenly misting up.

"What's the matter? Something went wrong, didn't it?"

Elise nodded.

"Was I killed? I couldn't have been killed. I'm here. But this is before then. I was killed when I went back. Is that what you're trying to tell me?"

Elise shook her head, afraid to speak.

Chris was confused. "For God's sake, what is it?"

"You weren't in the battle."

"I wasn't in the battle?" He stopped. "I don't understand. If I wasn't in the battle, and I wasn't killed before it, then where was I?"

"Here."

There was a pause, then, "Are you trying to confuse me?" Another moment passed, then his face lit up. "The battle... it's going on right now?"

Elise nodded as she turned her head to face him again. "In

a sense, yes. The battle is going on in its slot in time."

"But if I'm here…"

"You disappeared just before the battle started. When Colonel Custer couldn't find you, he declared you a deserter and had someone else lead your column."

Chris was shocked. "A deserter! Me? But I didn't desert. You took me away!"

Elise shivered as her eyes welled up with tears. "I'm sorry," she whispered.

"Sorry?" Chris stood up. "Sorry? I'm a deserter from the U.S. Army, and you're sorry?"

Their attention was jerked away when Richard suddenly burst in the room. "I thought I told you to lock this door." He paused. "Hey, what's going on?"

Chris sank slowly back onto the couch. Richard looked at Elise and understood. "I'm sorry," he said.

"Everybody's sorry," Chris muttered.

Elise looked at Chris. "If you were to return, it would upset history. There's no telling what changes might occur. Perhaps I might never have been born."

"Sounds like a personal problem to me." Chris sounded bitter.

"Now look," Richard broke in, "it's not our fault that you're here either. It was an act of God, fate, call it what you like, but it's not our fault."

Chris looked up; his eyes clouded over. "That doesn't help me, does it? Not one damn bit."

"Look," Richard suggested, "we're all tired. We've all been through a lot today. Why don't we all go to bed and get some rest. Tomorrow we can decide what to do. Captain, I know how you must feel, but we couldn't send you back tonight however badly we wanted to."

Chris didn't answer.

"Elise, do you have any extra blankets?"

"Yes." She rose to get them.

Richard turned to Chris. "Captain, you've got to understand

that what happened was beyond our control. What ever happened, happened. All we can do now is try to make the best of a bad situation. Can you understand this?"

"Do I have a choice?"

It was Richard's turn not to answer. He left the captain and joined Elise at the closet. "Do you think he'll be all right?" he whispered.

"Under the circumstances, I'd say he's taking it very well, considering we've destroyed him. You should have seen his eyes when I told him what had happened to him. He can't believe that he's been branded as a deserter."

"Does he know that he can't go back?"

Elise closed her eyes and leaned against the closet door. "He knows. At least I told him. I'm sure he can't accept it yet."

Richard leaned back and glanced at the captain, still sitting on the couch. "He's awfully depressed. You don't think he might..."

Elise shook her head. "I think he's stronger than that, although I don't see how."

They took the blankets into the living room.

"Okay Captain, the couch is all yours." Richard tried to sound cheerful.

Chris stared at him with red eyes.

Richard took a deep breath. "Captain, promise me that you won't run away tonight."

Chris looked Richard square in the eyes. "Where would I go?" he said simply. "Where would I go?"

CHAPTER 5

A few minutes before the sun dipped its shining head below the skyline, James and Gregory stepped out of their second story room at the Royal Palms Motel. Gregory shut the door and adjusted the broken plastic number '22'.

"Hey, James, why don't we move outta this dump?"

James picked a small piece of lint from his coat sleeve. "My friend, it is written that the meek shall inherit the earth. We shall live in humble dwellings until the time we can afford better. We are, at the moment..." he waved his hand through the air, "oh, what is the expression?"

"Broke?"

"Precisely." He started down the chipped cement steps.

Each of them carried a brown paper grocery bag containing wallets and purses, tels and keycards, stolen yesterday, to be returned today for a reward. Any jewelry found was fenced, any cash, spent. They got into their older model red Chevrolet. James usually drove because he enjoyed the challenge of city traffic and Gregory was lousy at it. As he backed around in the parking lot and headed towards the exit, Gregory pointed up at the dilapidated motel sign.

"Hey, the vacancy sign is on again. You didn't forget to pay our rent again, did you?"

James glanced at Gregory, then up at the flashing neon sign.

Rooms – Day – Week – Monthly – Rates. Underneath that was the vacancy sign. Some of the letters didn't light up and it read, V CANC. "You don't suppose that nice Thelma Margason moved out from next door, do you? I certainly hope not. She has so many nice things."

Gregory agreed, "Yeah, at least she did until we moved in."

They drove with the windows down. It was a very warm evening, and their car had no air conditioning.

"Ah, Gregory, just smell that fresh summer air," James breathed deeply and coughed.

"Yeah," commented Gregory, "another crystal smogged evening."

James drove them quickly to the first address on their list. It was going to be a busy evening.

They walked together up the front walk to the door through a small, but well-kept yard. James knocked on the door and put on an ingratiating smile.

A young woman, pleasantly dressed, answered the door. "May I help you?"

"Excuse us for bothering you," James said, "but are you Nancy Patton?"

"Yes."

"Well, we found something that I believe belongs to you." He held up her purse.

"Why, that's my purse!"

"We found it near the park, downtown, this afternoon."

Nancy Patton looked at the two well-dressed gentlemen smiling at her. "Why, thank you. It was stolen from me yesterday." She smiled.

"We found it tossed in some bushes. We were sure you would want whatever papers you might happen to have in it," James told her. "Are you missing any money or credit cards?"

Nancy looked and frowned. "Yes, I had several dollars, and that's gone, but all my credit cards are here... and my driver's license. How can I thank you? I was really upset over losing my license and cards. I worry so much about identity theft. Let me get you a reward."

James held up his hands. "A reward is totally unnecessary. We're only glad to have been able to return what we did. Our reward is your happiness."

And the fifty dollars that had been in the purse, Gregory thought.

"No, I insist," Nancy said. "Wait right here." She disappeared inside the house to return a moment later with a twenty-dollar bill. "Here, my husband insists that you take this."

James put up a mild protest but gave up finally and accepted the money. They left the happy lady and returned to their car. "Isn't it a good feeling to be charitable?" James asked.

Gregory thought so, too, and replied, "Why, yes, yes, it is."

They drove to three more addresses and repeated their 'charitable' act. As they drove around, Gregory turned on one of the tels that they had stolen. "Well, what's new in the news today?" James asked.

Gregory checked a news feed. "There was a mugging in the park this afternoon."

"You don't say."

"And here's a story about that nut shootin' his gun downtown."

"Happens all the time." James pulled into the evening traffic.

Gregory stared at the display. "It looks like the president's foreign policy on domestic issues is working… unemployment is at an all-time high."

James frowned, curled his lip, and slowly shook his head. "Somehow, I don't think you fully grasp that story."

Gregory wasn't bothered. "It seems like the big news is that they tested some kind of new time machine."

"Why is that the big news?"

"It's all over the news feed."

James was confused. "If it's all over the news feed, why do you read it last?"

Gregory had an answer. "I always start at the little stories.

The big stories always have the same depressing news. Crime, crime, crime."

"I see."

Gregory was silent for a moment, reading. "Now, this is an interesting item. The Chief of Police says he's gonna crack down on small time crime."

"An honorable gesture."

"I always thought them guys at City Hall should earn their money..." He didn't finish because James suddenly slammed on the brakes, screeching to a complete stop in the middle of traffic. There was a small chain reaction behind them. Horns began honking. James rolled up his window. Gregory got a nasty bump from hitting his head on the dashboard.

"What did... what did we hit?" he asked.

"What did you say?" James demanded.

Someone knocked on James' window. James locked his door and repeated his question. "What did you say?"

Gregory's eyes rolled. "I said, what did we hit?"

The guy outside stuck his head in the back window. "Get this hunk 'o junk off the street!" he shouted.

James ignored him. "Before that," he said to Gregory.

Gregory rubbed the knot on his head gingerly. "Uh... the Chief of Police says that he's gonna..."

The guy had the back door open now. "Are you gonna move this heap or do I?" he screamed.

"Before that," James said impatiently. Cars were backed up for a block behind them, honking, trying to get around them.

Gregory thought for a moment. "Gee, I don't remember."

The guy in the back shouted in James' ear. "If you don't move this car before I count three..."

James shushed him. "Just a minute, please!" He turned back to Gregory. "About a time machine," he prodded.

"Let's see, it's here someplace." Gregory tried to open the news feed again.

The guy in the back threw up his hands, got out, slammed the door, and marched back to his own car.

"Yeah, here it is," Gregory said as he scrolled down, "Big headlines. World's First Time Machine Tested. Director of General Amalgamated Laboratories, Dr. Marvin Bruce... hey the guy's got a first name for his last name!"

"Never mind that!"

"Oh, yeah, Doctor Bruce announced today the experimental testing of the world's first time travel vehicle. This guy, Bruce, expressed disappointment over a small malfunction during today's test which caused the experiment to abort early. Tests are being run to date dust samples gathered for conclusive proof that the vehicle did pass back in time. Project Director, Dr. Elise McAllister, was unavailable for comment."

"That's it!" James shouted as he suddenly spun the car around in a sharp U-turn, causing three more fender benders.

"That's what?" Gregory struggled to sit up.

"This morning, downtown, remember?"

Gregory was confused. He thought for a moment, then, "Yes, of course! I do remember being downtown this morning!" He paused. "So what?"

James wheeled through traffic back towards their apartment. "I'm a fool!"

Gregory wasn't sure how to answer that, so he didn't comment.

"I don't know why it didn't hit me at the time," James said. "There it was in black and white, and I let it pass right by. Just right by."

"Let what pass right by?"

James smiled secretly. "Opportunity, my dear fellow. Opportunity knocks but once. We much reach out and grab it while we have the chance."

Gregory didn't have the slightest idea what James was carrying on about. He had never seen his partner so excited about anything before. Whatever he had in mind must be big... and whenever James had big ideas, it usually revolved around money. Gregory smiled, too.

James drove as fast as he dared, weaving in and out of

traffic, until, at last, he pulled back into their motel parking lot. "We were on the next block over from General Amalgamated Laboratories this morning, remember?" He grabbed his sack of wallets and ran up the steps to their apartment. Gregory followed silently, curiously. He still didn't understand. James ran to the kitchen and grabbed an old coffee container full of keycards. "These keycards, do you remember them?" He picked up a set from the top.

Gregory took them and inspected them carefully. "Sure, I remember them. I took them from that guy in the white lab coat downtown."

James stared at him. "Don't you realize what we've got here?"

Gregory nodded. "A set of keys from a guy in a white lab coat downtown this morning."

"Two and two," James said exasperated, "just put together two and two!"

Gregory scrunched up his face in thought for a moment, then smiled. "Four," then he frowned. "You got four keys? That ain't right. There are six keys on that ring."

James snatched the keys back from Gregory. "What we have here, you idiot, is the key to our future. Can't you figure out where these keys came from?"

Gregory didn't like being talked to in this way, and he was getting mad. "I already told you where they came from. The guy in the white lab coat this morning!"

"These keys are from General Amalgamated Laboratories."

Gregory stopped short. "Hey, that's where they tested that new time machine, ain't it?"

James smiled benevolently at his partner. "Sometimes you simply amaze me, my friend. And look here.... a security card, too."

Gregory blushed. "Aw, it's nuttin', really."

"You can say that again."

"This could be the biggest thing in our career."

"Unquestionably."

Gregory's eyes sparkled as he thought of the prospects. The visions in his mind were of a heist so grand, so magnificent; "We steal the time machine!" he said.

James slapped his hand to his forehead, closed his eyes, and counted to ten. "We don't steal the time machine," he said tightly.

"We don't?" Gregory was confused. The visions in his mind had been of lifting the giant machine, at least he guessed it was a giant machine, out of the laboratory and... he didn't know exactly what next, but that was a minor point. With these keys, they could get in the building and... "We don't?"

"No, we don't," James said wearily.

Gregory pursed his lips, then brightened. "Of course, we don't. That was a silly idea, wasn't it?"

James nodded. Gregory waited.

At length, James explained. "We steal the plans for the time machine, not the machine itself. I think it is safe to assume the plans are probably on a memory card or set of cards. I would guess there are multiple sets in case something happens to the original. We go get one of the duplicate card sets. It will be less noticeable that way, give us some time to make our sale.

"You know," Gregory said nodding in agreement, "I was just thinkin' along those very same lines," he said slowly.

"I had no doubts."

"Who do we sell the cards to? I don't remember Harry ever fencing anything like that before."

Why? What did I ever do to deserve this, James wondered as he looked at Gregory and channeled his irritation to patience. "We don't fence it locally. I'll wager that there are foreign countries that would give their right upper arm for those plans. Especially since we know the thing works. They would gladly hand over their treasuries..." He broke off in awe of his own plan.

"We could give up picking pockets," Gregory said.

"Forever."

"My mother would be so proud. She's wanted me to give it

up for some time now."

"A dear lady," James smiled. "We have plans to plan, tel
calls to make, materials to buy…"

CHAPTER 6

Elise rolled over in her bed and groggily reached for her alarm clock. Through sleepy eyes, she saw the time. Six-fifteen a.m. She yawned a long, lingering yawn as she reached for her robe, then staggered hazily through the bedroom into the living room. Richard lay curled up in a most uncomfortable looking position in the oversized chair, snoring lightly. Elise glanced at the pile of covers on the couch. A pile of covers was all it was.

"Richard, wake up! He's gone!" She was fully awake now. "Richard, Captain Garrett ran away again!"

"Yeah, yeah, I'll get up in a minute," he mumbled as he rolled, repositioning himself to stretch his cramped muscles.

Elise yanked the covers off him.

"What is it?" he asked, trying to focus his eyes. "Where am I, anyway?"

"Captain Garrett is gone!" Elise said again, only this time twice as loud.

Richard sat up, struggling to awaken fully. "Gone? Where could he go? He promised he wouldn't."

"Promise or no promise, he's gone. Get dressed. We're going to have to go find him before he gets into some serious trouble." Elise started back towards the bedroom.

Richard had slept with his pants and tee shirt on. He grabbed his socks. "Where are we going to look?" he asked.

Elise yelled from the bedroom. "I suppose we should start

with the park. It's familiar territory to him now."

Richard didn't see how the captain could possibly find his way back there, but he had, in fact, found it once already. "Good as any," he mumbled as he struggled into his shirt.

Elise hurried into the living room all dressed. "I wish I knew what we were going to do with him once we find him, but I guess we'll worry about that when the time comes."

They stepped out into the hall and quickly walked to the elevator. Elise stopped short and stared at the elevator floor light. It was on two, then shot up to eighty-seven, then back down to five, and quickly up to one hundred, then down to one. Elise frowned and pushed the down button as the elevator zoomed by them on its way to ninety-six. A moment later, the doors opened in front of them.

"Well, good mornin'," Chris drawled. "It's about time you two sleepyheads got up." His face was flush with excitement.

Elise and Richard looked at each other. Elise rolled her eyes and Richard burst into laughter.

"Like the man says, you've got to make the best of a bad situation," Chris laughed. "This here is quite the contraption. But how does everybody in this building use this thing at the same time? And where are they all?"

Elise grabbed him by the arm and pulled him out of the elevator, and down the hall. "They don't all use this one. There are many elevators for each floor. We've just been lucky so far that no one has been using this particular one when you were around. I think you'd better stay inside until we figure a way to spring you on civilization," she said with a sidelong glance.

Safely back in the apartment, Chris began rubbing his stomach. "When does the chow wagon open up around here? A man could starve."

Richard thumped him good naturedly on the shoulder. "How could you be hungry after all the excitement you've had? Besides, you had a hot dog yesterday. We didn't even get ours."

Chris looked at Richard. "How do you know about that?"

Richard smiled.

"You really eat those things?" Chris asked.

"It's the great American pastime," Richard said. "Baseball, Mom's apple pie, and hot dogs."

"It is amazing how things change," Chris said. "When I was… I mean back home… anyway, only Indians eat dog meat."

Elise choked in the kitchen. "Dog meat!"

"Yeah," Chris said, "that's why I was kind of surprised to find people trading for it."

"Dog meat?" Richard was puzzled. "You mean you thought a hot dog was made out of dog meat? Yuk!"

Now Chris was puzzled. "Well, isn't it?"

Richard laughed until he was out of breath and had to sit down. "They're not any kind of meat. Soybeans and artificial flavorings and coloring…" he broke off laughing again.

Elise stuck her head through the kitchen doorway. "Captain, perhaps you'd like to clean up before we eat. Breakfast will be ready shortly."

Chris could already smell the prepared biscuits in the oven. He looked at his dirty uniform and smiled. "I guess I could use a little cleanin' up."

Elise pointed through the bedroom to the bathroom. "It's in there."

Chris craned his neck. "What's in there?" he asked.

"The bathroom… you know, and the toilet."

Chris stared at her.

Elise bit her tongue to keep from laughing. "Richard, would you be so kind as to demonstrate to the captain the many conveniences we enjoy in our modern bathrooms?"

Richard jumped to his feet. "Follow me, Captain."

Chris stared at himself in the floor to ceiling mirrors that dominated the far wall of the brightly lit bathroom. He scarcely heard Richard's spiel on the advancements made in the way of toilets that flush (he had relieved himself at the police station last night, but didn't know about flushing), hot and cold running water, and the directions of the tub/shower combination. He searched his reflection in the huge mirror for any physical changes to match the mental trauma that shaken him so badly in the past twenty-four hours.

"Just remember," Richard was saying, "the cold is on the right and the hot is on the left. Here's a towel."

Chris took the fluffy blue towel and stared blankly at Richard.

"You all right?"

Chris focused. "Yeah, fine. Just thinking."

Richard smiled. "We'll be right out here if you need anything."

Chris nodded and sat on the toilet to take off his boots. Richard left the room, closing the door behind him. Chris finished undressing and stepped into the shower. Hot and cold. Amazing. He turned the hot water on full. 'A nice warm bath sounds good,' he thought to himself.

"Do you think he's all right?" Richard asked Elise as she pulled the biscuits out of the oven and upon hearing a painful yelp from the bathroom.

"Right now, or over all?"

"Overall."

Elise thought for a moment before answering. "Everything we've seen so far points to a very mature man adjusting quite well, even remarkably, to an untested situation. His actions and reactions seem quite normal."

"But he still thinks he's going back."

Elise looked at him. "Why do you say that? Has he mentioned it already this morning?"

"Not specifically, but just now, in the bathroom, I could see in his eyes that he was someplace else." He picked up a biscuit but dropped it because it was hot. "Maybe I'm seeing something that isn't there."

"It's difficult to say," Elise agreed. "Yesterday, I wanted nothing more than to send him right back. It can't be done. I know that, but it took me a while to accept it. Let's hope the captain accepts it soon, too."

Nothing else was said while Elise went about preparing breakfast. Chris joined them in a few minutes.

They sat down to a meal of biscuits, eggs, bacon, hash browns and coffee. Chris' eyes lit up when he saw the spread on the table, then he frowned. "Is any of this real food?"

Elise laughed. "It's all real, Captain."

They all dug in hungrily. Chris asked a steady stream of questions about life in his future. Elise and Richard did their best to explain without getting technical, and found it was difficult to do. Elise noted that Chris never once asked about what happened in the period of time right after he was taken from the Montana Territory. It was as if he had forgotten that he had been with Custer, but she knew it would come up soon enough.

"So, everybody has this e-lectric-isity?" Chris asked.

"We couldn't live without it," Richard said. "Just about everything runs on it. Some from solar, some from wind and nuclear power. We use it for lights, heat, cooling, cooking..."

Chris took another biscuit and began mopping his plate with it. "I don't know if I could understand all this if I stayed here for a hundred years. It sure all is something."

"Those clothes you're wearing sure are something, too," Elise said. "We've got to get you something else. I didn't even think of it before."

Chris brushed at his shirt. "Oh, that's all right. I can just wash these out and they'll be fine."

"I don't think they're quite in style at the moment," Elise said. "I'm pretty sure I can fix you up, though."

Chris shook his head. "You're crazier than a lame prairie dog if you think I've got a mind to wear your clothes. I'd sooner go without... beggin' your pardon."

Elise laughed. "Not my clothes - my father's."

Chris looked at Richard.

"My father died about a year ago," Elise explained. "I couldn't bring myself to throw out his things. He was a big man, so maybe something of his will fit. All we can do is try."

Richard glanced at his watch. "Hey, we've got to get to the office. It's getting late!" He looked at Elise.

She nodded. "Except we can't exactly take the captain with us."

"We'll have to take turns staying with him," Richard said. "Why don't I go down to the office and work with Wende for a while... say, until lunch. Then you can go in."

Chris scratched his chin. "Why does anybody have to stay with me? I'm a real big boy now. I can take pretty good care of myself."

"It's not that," Elise assured him. "We're still not sure what effects the molecular transfer may have had on your systems. There could be some delayed side effects. We want to be with you just in case."

Chris started to protest but thought better of it and simply shrugged.

Richard finished his coffee. "I'll be back around lunch time. If anything happens, call me."

"We may go out to get the captain some clothes," Elise said, "but we should be back before noon."

Richard grabbed the last biscuit and left.

Chris pushed himself away from the table with a groan. "I may have changed some," he said, "but my stomach sure ain't got no bigger. I'm stuffed. You could have fed a whole regiment with all that breakfast." He fell silent.

Elise caught his silence and was afraid he was going to start asking questions about his comrades. "Well, if you are all finished, why don't we see about getting you a change of clothes."

Chris looked at her and winked. She felt a chill go up her back. "Let's see what you've got," he said.

He followed her into the bedroom and watched her rummage through some boxes pulled from the closet. This stuff, cardboard, that the boxes were made of was really something, but then, everything was really something. Finally, Elise decided on a light blue pinstripe suit with wide lapels.

"Here," she said. "Try this on for size. I'll wait in the living room."

Chris waited until she closed the door, then held up the suit.

Elise sat on the couch and pondered the next move. She probably should have gone into the lab herself first this morning, but she was reluctant to leave the Captain. Oh, well, she would get him outfitted, and then go to the office this afternoon. Richard and Wende could cover for her until then... she hoped.

The bedroom door opened, and Chris stepped out into the living room. Elise collapsed in laughter in spite of herself. Pinstripe suit, pants tucked inside his dirty black boots, white shirt with sleeves too long, necktie tied into a draping bow around his neck, and floppy hat on his head. He smiled. "I didn't think much of the suit, myself."

Elise shook her head, grinning. "It's not the suit."

Chris frowned. "It's not?"

A little talking convinced him to take off his hat, try on a pair of regular shoes and fix his tie.

He tried the shoes. They were a little small, as was the rest of the suit. "How do you walk in these things?" He took a few steps gingerly.

"You won't have to wear this for long," she assured him. "At least now, you're only fifty years behind the fashions."

Chris wasn't sure what to think. He was mighty uncomfortable, but still, it was good to be out of that heavy, smelly old uniform.

Elise picked up her purse from alongside the bed. "Well, Captain, if you would be so kind as to join me, we're going to give you a look at the world... 2045 style."

They went in Elise's car. Chris was wary of riding in the vehicle, and doubly so at Elise driving, but he gave in at last. Elise drove him to a downtown shopping mall and parked far out in a crowded parking lot. Chris was nothing less than totally amazed at the number of cars and people. He stared at the covered people mover whisking people from the parking lot directly into the indoor mall. Elise had to take his arm and lead him hesitantly onto the moving belt. He chuckled as he stood still yet moved toward the building. To think of all the dirty, hard miles he had hiked and ridden, rain or shine. He couldn't even begin to properly imagine the mobilization of today's armies.

He stared wide-eyed as they entered the ante-arbor of the building. Large vents blew cool, refreshing air over them as they passed into the main hall of the mall. Chris had never seen so many people gathered together in one place in all his life. He reckoned there must be literally thousands of people inside this building.

The huge, brightly lit corridors were lined with hundreds of small shops. Each shop was heralded by gaily decorated and brightly lit signs proclaiming the name and probable contents of the particular store. Any conceivable item was for sale under one gigantic roof.

Now, Chris had been in a mercantile or two in his life, but nothing could have prepared him for the spectacle laid out before him. Elise let him stand for a few moments, eyes wide, trying to take in everything at once. His eyes, and Elise suspected, his mind, were in constant motion.

"It's quite a place," she remarked casually.

"I've never seen anything like it... so many shops..."

"This is the largest shopping mall in the world. Over two thousand shops offering everything from soup to nuts."

Chris stopped in front of a shop that specialized in kitchen utensils. He peered in the window display. Nothing looked like it might belong in any kitchen he had ever been in.

Elise pointed. "That's a blender, that's a toaster, there's an electric can opener."

Chris looked at her blankly.

"Let's find a clothing store."

Chris allowed himself to be led through the crowd, occasionally running up to a window, staring at the vast array of goods offered. He laughed and asked questions like a child about everything. What is this? What is that? What do you use these for? People actually wear those? Everything delighted him. He was lost in a new world, for a time, the past forgotten.

Elise felt her cheeks flush warmly as she suddenly realized that the feelings she had for Chris were not all pity and sorrow... or all scientific. He brought her strength, and maybe more.

She finally dragged him into a men's clothing store. The impeccably dressed clerk eyed them suspiciously, especially Chris.

"May I help you?"

"I need some duds," Chris told him.

The clerk's mustache twitched slightly. "Duds?"

Elise stepped forward. "We need to get a complete outfit for my... my..." My what?

Chris moved away, fascinated by the selection of colors and the types of materials. He fingered everything. He would pull a shirt from a rack, hold it up, and ask Elise, "What do you think?", then move on, leaving Elise to hang it up.

The clerk was obviously displeased with Chris' behavior.

"Did you actually wish to purchase something, or are you just here to fondle our material?"

"No, we need to get him some clothes," Elise assured him. She hung up the jacket that Chris had just left. "You see, we don't exactly know the size of my... my..."

Chris yahooed when he discovered a display of cowboy boots. The clerk rushed over to him, Elise right behind.

"Chris, why don't you let the gentleman take your measurements?" It was the first time she had called him by his first name. It felt good.

Chris smiled and winked at her, and she did something she hadn't done in a very long time. Elise blushed.

It took twenty minutes with the exasperated clerk before Chris was fitted for size, Chris slapping at the man as he tried to take measurements. Another half hour was spent in choosing clothing before they finally left the store. Chris was decked out as a sign of the times in a brown sports coat with tan slacks, striped shirt, and brown socks and shoes. Elise was surprised at how Chris kept his ruggedness despite the new clothes. Evidently, the Montana Territory had agreed with him.

"What time does the chuck wagon pull through?" Chris asked.

"You're hungry already?" Elise looked at her watch. It was almost eleven o'clock. "All right, let's grab a quick bite for lunch, then we've got to get back. What will it be? Chinese? Mexican? Italian?..." She broke off laughing when she saw Chris staring blankly at her again. "There's any kind of restaurant you want. Just name it." She waved her hand toward a row of eateries.

Chris thought for a moment. "A hot dog," he announced at length. "Does one of them places sell hot dogs?"

Elise laughed. "A hot dog? You've got every kind of international cuisine available, and you want a hot dog?"

Chris nodded eagerly. Elise rolled her eyes, took him by the arm and led him to the Dogie Korral.

"This time, we pay, okay?" she chuckled.

Chris laughed easily with her. "You pay. I don't exactly have anything to pay with." Then he frowned. "I don't even know how I'm going to pay you back," he said seriously.

"Don't worry, I'm a liberated woman."

"I thought you were a doctor."

They got their hot dogs and walked over to a small, green, park-like area in the center of the mall. They found a deserted bench and sat down. Chris took a bite of his hot dog and sat, chewing pensively.

"What am I doing here?" he asked.

Elise sighed. "It must be very difficult for you. I've been amazed at your strength in coping. I'm sure I couldn't do as well as you have given the same situation."

"At first, I thought I was going crazy. It's kind of hard to explain. There isn't any physical struggle, just in my head, you know? Yesterday (was it only yesterday?) is all lost to me. I don't remember much of it. I mean, it's kind of like a bein' a brand-new baby, if you know what I mean. One minute, you're an officer in the U.S. Army, and the next, you're just a child in a new world... all this is a new world. It's incredible. Nobody back there would believe me, that's for sure." Chris leaned back on the bench. "Back there. So far away. So long ago, yet I'm still an officer under General Custer's command. In a way, I need him, and he needs me. If I can get back, I'm leading a column..." He broke off in mid-sentence.

Elise looked into his troubled eyes. "You can't go back."

He looked sharply at her.

"Who are we to alter history? We can't change the past."

"You changed it," he said with a bite in his words. "You took me away from the battle. I'd call that changing things."

"We didn't change history. We were merely a means to carry out a plan that controls all our lives."

Chris was baffled. "I don't understand."

"I don't understand either. I doubt anyone really does or can. We didn't change history by bringing you here. It's in the history books that you did not participate in the battle of the Little Big Horn. Nothing is said about what happened to you, other than you just weren't there anymore."

"But it wasn't history yet when you took me," Chris argued. "The battle hadn't even taken place yet."

Elise looked patiently at him. "The fact that we took you away from the battle is why you didn't participate. There's a great deal unexplained. What I'm saying is, that even when we took you away, the battle had already taken place in its slot in time. Remember what I said before, the battle of the Little Big Horn is going on perpetually in its time slot. If this building were suddenly to collapse and kill everyone inside, it is already in the history pages of the future."

"I don't know," Chris said. "It's all a confusion to me."

"Of course, it is. We are just beginning to scratch the surface of understanding ourselves. My whole life has been devoted to studying time and its effects, and I don't understand. It's all theory so far. Yesterday's test was supposed to answer a lot of questions for us... it only brought more."

Chris looked at the crowd. "Do they all believe as you do?"

Elise shook her head. "No, I'm sure they don't. That's what makes people, people. You know, it's surprising, but with all of our technology; advances in power sources, machinery, computers, gadgets and gizmos, people are still people. They still eat, sleep, think, and make mistakes. It's all a master plan far beyond our understanding. You are living what no man probably should ever truly see... his own future. And yet, there must be a reason for it. Possibly you have some great contribution for our time."

"Then why wasn't I born in your time?"

"Who can say? Maybe you're a warning for us not to fool with the time frontier." Elise suddenly felt a chill. "Maybe some things are best left alone."

Chris shook his head doubtfully. "I just don't know. It don't make no sense to me. History that's history before it even happens, me being here..."

"Is it so bad being here?" Elise asked.

An answer didn't come right away. He closed his eyes thinking, mulling over his options, which pretty much amounted to none. "On one hand, I wish I had been left alone. I wasn't so miserable where I was. At least no more than anybody else." He took Elise's hand in his. "But then, I feel it was right. I can't explain it. It's like I'm supposed to be here... and I'm sorta glad I am here. You know, I have an idea that things always seem to work themselves out for the best."

Elise smiled.

Chris gazed into her dark eyes.

Impulsively, they were drawn into each other's arms. Chris lifted her chin and gently kissed her. She kissed him back. Worlds apart were drawn together in a mutual understanding of human sensitivity.

"Welcome to 2045," Elise said, smiling.

Chris smiled back at her. "The future doesn't seem so bad, after all."

They kissed again, swept away in a timeless moment in time.

When they moved apart, both of them were suddenly aware of a small audience. Two children were standing, staring at them. Elise looked at the older of the two, a girl who was about six or seven years old.

"Hello."

We're lost," the little girl said. "And we don't know what time it is."

Chris picked up her little brother and sat him on his knee. "Well honey, I guess it's you and me against the world."

Richard sat on Elise's couch at her apartment and filled her in on all the details of the tests he and Wende had been running so far that morning. "I just can't believe that we haven't run across something yet," he said scratching his head. "Everything checks out perfectly. It's nothing less than incredible."

"Did you hear from Dr. Bruce?" Elise asked.

"Not yet, but I'm sure you will before the afternoon is over. I'm glad you're here to talk to him. So far, he doesn't even know that you weren't here this morning. We had to lock the doors to keep the press out. We told them that you were busy and couldn't be disturbed."

Elise nodded in relief. "Thanks. I'd better get on down there before somebody figures out that I'm missing. I trust that you and Chris can keep yourselves entertained for the rest of the afternoon?"

Richard smiled as he picked up the remote. "Do you know how long it's been since I've watched a soap opera? I'll fill the captain with all the glorious benefits of television."

Elise told them that she would be back in time for dinner and left. Richard to Chris. "Captain, prepare yourself for a dubious treat."

Chris sat up quickly. "ABBI, show me pictures!" Nothing

happened. "ABBI!"

Richard had to laugh in spite of himself. "Your voice print isn't keyed in yet."

Chris looked lost. "What does that even mean?"

"Don't worry," Richard assured him, "we'll get you dialed up and keyed in as soon as we get some of this other stuff sorted out."

Elise drove straight to the laboratory. There were only a couple of news people waiting outside the lab, and they didn't even recognize her as she unlocked the door and went in.

Wende was seated at her computer console deep in thought. She looked up when Elise cleared her throat behind her. "Oh, Elise, I didn't even hear you come in," she said. "How did you get past all the newsfeed people?"

"There were only a few of them left, and they didn't even know who I was. Where are we?"

Wende told her pretty much the same things Richard had, plus the results of the last few tests she had run. Everything checked out perfectly. It was frustrating that nothing seemed to be wrong. Elise wanted to redo a couple of the more complicated tests, and so they both set to work. There was a short interruption when Wende had some lunch sent up, but otherwise they were undisturbed until late in the afternoon when ABBI softly announced, "Incoming call for Elise." She answered it from her office and Dr. voice boomed out.

"Doctor McAllister?"

"Yes, doctor."

"What's going on down there? Why don't I have a report on my desk yet?" His voice sounded gruff, and he was definitely frowning.

"We don't have anything to report. We're still reviewing the data to try to find out what happened."

Doctor Bruce snorted. "The dating test results are in from the dust samples on the capsule. The dust is approximately one hundred years old."

Elise wanted to tell him that it was one hundred- and sixty-nine-year-old dust from the Montana Territory, but she kept silent.

"Congratulations on a successful test," he said hesitantly.

Elise was surprised. Congratulations from Doctor Bruce? And on a test that malfunctioned? He knew they were supposed to go back almost three hundred years.

"Doctor, you're not taking any of this work home to work on, are you? I mean, I know there was a slight malfunction, but it's absolutely necessary that nothing, absolutely nothing, leave the lab. Do you understand me?"

Not take anything home? Was this the tyrant Dr. Bruce talking? This wasn't at all like him.

"But, sir, it's imperative that we find the cause of the malfunction. We can't continue testing until…"

Doctor Bruce cut her off. "Let's take our time and be thorough. You've all been working very hard down there. I repeat myself; nothing leaves that lab tonight. No notes, nothing. Understood?"

Elise mumbled her assent.

"Let me know as soon as you find anything," Doctor Bruce growled, and cut her off.

Elise walked back into the lab quietly.

"Our illustrious leader?" Wende asked.

Elise nodded.

"That bad?"

Elise wasn't sure. "He congratulated us. And he thinks we've been working too hard, so he wants us to take our time finding out what went wrong."

Wende winced. "That's bad."

"It was surreal."

Doctor Bruce sat in his office, thinking. The test had not been a complete success, but they had conclusive proof that the capsule had traveled back in time. He knew that they were very close to achieving complete control in time travel. This should be an exciting time. He wiped his eyes. He hated to rush things, but the pressure being applied on him was making him a sick man. He was going to have to act soon. He could use the money to go on a nice, long vacation. He asked ABBI to get him a memorized number.

A man's voice answered. "It's cold out."

Doctor Bruce responded without hesitation. "It's summer."

"Go ahead," the voice said.

Doctor Bruce took a deep breath. "Tonight. Tonight, is the night."

The receiver clicked in his ear.

It was done.

CHAPTER 7

Wende's eyes began to water. It had been several hours since Elise had left, and she'd been working for hours before Elise had even shown up. Wende had insisted on staying and working for a while longer. It had seemed like a noble gesture at the time, but now her eyes hurt, and she was hungry. She thought of Elise, Richard, and the captain enjoying a nice, big dinner at Elise's apartment. Maybe she should have stopped to eat.

She felt more confident about doing the system checks on her own now that Elise had double checked some of the more critical ones and had come up with the same annoying 'System Nominal' results. Everything was frustratingly normal. The capsule shouldn't have malfunctioned. Checking all the memory programs for data deviation was a long and tedious job, and working alone was boring, but Wende plodded on.

She was glad that the captain had been found safe and sound and had seemed to settle down and accept his fate. Poor guy must really feel out of it, she thought. Things were in enough of a flap over the malfunction. If news of the captain got out, it would only lead to disaster. She had taken care to hide the closed-circuit digital recordings showing Captain Garrett, but she knew that they would eventually be found.

Luckily for Wende, that was Elise's problem.

The last of the program software was ready to be gone through. There had to be some deviations somewhere. Possibilities for malfunction flashed through Wende's mind, but the late hour was having its effects, and she was beginning to have trouble sorting out facts. As a last resort, she decided to get the master set of program plans from Elise's office. They were stored on memory string. Maybe an overall look at the schematics would spark some new ideas in her quest for something wrong.

She went into Elise's office and knelt down by the floor vault. There were only four keys to this vault. She had one, Richard, Elise, and, of course, Dr. Bruce had one. Poor Richard had lost his keys, and they still weren't found. Pity him when Dr. Bruce found out. She had thought it odd when Dr. Bruce insisted on only one master program memory string be made. Memory string technology was brand new. Quantum terabytes of information could be stored on memory string, embedded in a helix around the entire string. It frightened her to think what would happen if something happened to that one tiny string. All the hard drives of all the computers that the original programs had been designed on had been erase, and there was no cloud back-up, either... some story about how even military grade encryption could be hacked and this information was just too important to lose. But on the other hand, there was also less chance of the string being read by the wrong people if no more than one was even available. Business espionage was a constant threat. Other companies would be thrilled to have any of the information stored on this short length of string, although most of them wouldn't even have the technology to read it That's why access was limited to the four herself, Elise, Richard and, of course, Dr. Bruce. The less people looking at a master memory string, the better.

Wende was constantly aware of the enormous amount of responsibility she carried by being one of only those four people with access to the string. She took out the small rectangular box containing the string and closed the vault. Back in the lab, she carefully inserted the string into a complex reader.

A tree of schematics began to flash on her floating display as she put on her headset and touch gloves. She studied the listings, typed commands, and searched the information for a clue... any clue. Twenty minutes of intense studying only managed to give her a headache. She massaged her temples, but the dull pain would not go away. Perhaps some water splashed on her face would wake her up and make her feel better.

She removed her headset and gloves and walked slowly into the anteroom. The building was empty, except for herself, and it seemed oddly quiet. Wende was used to action and noise going on constantly in and around the lab. She ran some cold water and listened to it splashing in the sink. She wet a paper towel and crossed to the couch. Visions of Captain Garrett filled her mind. She could still see him lying on the couch, unconscious, handsome. She laid down and put the towel over her face to rest for a few minutes. Her mind was crowded with diagrams, figures, and thoughts of the captain. She dozed fitfully for a few minutes. Fearful that she would fall asleep right there, she sat up. She spotted Captain Garrett's sword and gun belt hanging from a hook near the closet. Richard had hung it there when he took the weapons from the captain yesterday.

Wende rose to look closely at the sword scabbard. This thing is heavy, she thought as she lifted the belt from the hook. He packed this thing around all day? No wonder he's so muscular. She pulled the sword from the ornate scabbard. It was actually a French mounted artillery saber. It had a long-curved blade, a narrow hilt, and a brass guard. She absently fingered the blade while a fantasy of being a damsel in distress saved by the gallant, handsome cavalry officer went through her mind.

She was being held captive in the tall tower of a fortress by a horrible man with a mustache. The horrible man with the mustache wanted her to marry him, but she would not give in.

She hated mustaches. She was kept in a small computer cubicle and forced to work on complicated programs all day until she broke down. But she refused to break down, for she knew that one day, a handsome cavalry officer would appear on a white horse with brown spots on its back, and rescue her. And sure enough, one day, Captain Garrett appeared on such a beautiful horse. He looked dashing in his long, blue tailcoat and shiny black boots. She was wearing her new skirt with the matching short waist jacket… her peach one. He rode up in a cloud of dust, shouted, "Whoa, Thunder!" and looked up at her window. One look was all it took. He was in love with her. He started up the long, winding stairs of the tower, but the horrible man with the mustache tried to stop him. A fight ensued, fast and furious, over her. Of course, the gallant Captain was victorious. He broke down the door to her small computer cubicle and bore her away…

Wende blinked and slowly, reluctantly, returned to reality. She slid the saber back into its scabbard and rubbed her eyes, surprised at how much effort it took to reopen them. Fatigue was really getting to her, and no wonder. It was already after midnight. Fatigue was definitely not what she needed right now. That's what would cause her to make mistakes, and mistakes couldn't be tolerated now. Time was too precious.

She took the sword and holster belt back into the lab with her. Fortunately, no one in the press had mentioned the sword, or even seemed interested in it, but then, there were various other artifacts lying around the anteroom. No one would have any reason to suspect where the sword came from… until someone sees the recorded image files, she thought. Then it's going to hit the fan.

She leaned the sword up against the computer, not wanting to give up her fantasy just yet. She stared at the holo display. Details of complex circuitry for the capsule stared back at her. Her eyes were tired and the lines on the screen began to turn fuzzy and blur together. After five minutes, she realized that she was getting too tired to continue much longer. She was only going to miss something, and then they would have to repeat everything she was doing anyway. She took the memory string out of the reader and carefully set it on the ledge just above the sword. There was one more program that she wanted to check, then she would give up for the night and put everything away.

She turned to the display to her left and asked ABBI for a command. Numbers and symbols flashed in front of her. She studied them. Nothing. Everything was normal. Wende never thought she'd be disappointed by something being so darned normal, but she was disappointed now. Discouraged, she slammed down her tablet and put her head down to pout, her eyes closed.

Thus, unseen to her, the small gust of wind caused by her slamming the tablet down, blew the memory string off its precarious perch and carried it gently downward. The string hit the saber hilt and quickly slid down into the scabbard, and out of sight.

Wende awoke with a start. She blinked her eyes furiously, trying to clear them. Where was she? Slowly, her bearings came to her, and she realized that she had fallen asleep across her tablet. She looked at her watch. one o'clock in the morning! She had been asleep for over thirty minutes. Quickly, she gathered her papers together. She reached to pull the memory string from the reader, but the reader was empty. Smiling to herself, she remembered that she had taken it out already and laid it… The memory string was gone! Surely, she hadn't already put it away. No. She fought to remember as she frantically searched the floor. She had put the string on this small ledge while she ran the last program review. This, she remembered clearly and distinctly, only now it wasn't there. She dropped to her knees and searched everywhere, but to no avail. The memory string had simply, seemingly, disappeared. A feeling of panic began to choke her as she came to the conclusion that the string was no longer in the room. Could someone possibly have come into the room while she dozed, and taken it?

Thirty minutes of fruitless searching only shook Wende's faith in the belief of a benevolent deity. She didn't smoke or drink or carouse around. She paid her taxes. She even paid her tel bill on time. So, why? Why this, to her? What had she done to deserve... her eyes lit up as a thought occurred to her. The sword! Perhaps the string had somehow fallen into the scabbard. Quickly she pulled the sword out and shook the scabbard upside down. She pounded it on the floor, but never once did she notice the missing length of magnetic string clinging stubbornly, tightly to the sword blade, out of her sight. In exasperation, she stuffed the saber back in the scabbard. Now, what? How was she going to explain this? "I'm sorry, Dr. Bruce, I seem to have lost the world's only complete set of plans to the time travel vehicle." What else? She looked around. There was always the time capsule. Maybe she could escape to another time. Her head began to throb. Obviously, the thing to do was to calm down. Composing herself, she took out a tissue and shakily wiped perspiration from her brow. Dr. Bruce's wrath would be unbearable.

The solution she finally decided upon was to go home, get some rest, and return in a few hours to continue searching. If she still couldn't find the string, she would face the music like a woman... if she decided to stay in the country.

"James! James, wake up!" Gregory had been dozing himself, and almost missed seeing the lights go out high in the laboratory building. They were parked a couple of blocks away from the General Amalgamated Laboratories where they wouldn't attract attention to themselves but could still clearly see the building. He quickly got out of the car, calling to James all the time. "James, wake up. James, now's our chance. Come on, James."

James shifted uncomfortably in his seat. Sleeping in the driver's seat of a car was not just uncomfortable, it was insufferable. Cramps, kinks, cricks, pangs, tickles, and spasms plagued his body as he tried to position himself in even a semirecumbent pose. Gads, did these people work around the clock?

"James, wake up!"

James suddenly sat straight up in the seat, his eyes wide open. "Yes, I'm here. What is it?"

"All the lights are out in the building," Gregory told him.

"Lights?"

"Yeah, everybody's gone…" Gregory looked into James' blank face and realized that he was still sleeping. "James…"

"Never go home…"

"James!" Gregory suddenly shouted.

James snapped awake. "It's time," he announced as though he had been leading the conversation all along. "We go with Plan A."

"But nobody's going to be in the building with all the lights turned off," Gregory protested.

James shook his head. "We can't be sure until we execute Plan A. We must be certain that no one remains inside. Let's move the car closer."

Gregory sighed and got back into the car. There was a sack of pocket tels in the backseat. They could use one to execute Plan A. It was a deceptively simple plan. They would call the lab to see if anyone answered the tel. No answer, no problem. James started the car and pulled away from the curb to park across from the front of the building just as Wende pulled up onto the street from the underground parking lot. Her lights caught James and Gregory broadside as they pulled up. She was too tired and worried to recognize the fact that it was an odd time for a car to be pulling up in front of the lab, and she only unconsciously recorded it.

James shut off the engine and turned off the lights. "Where is the laboratory number? I wrote it down."

Gregory shrugged. "I don't know. Maybe it's in your wallet."

James pulled out his wallet. "It's not here," he announced a moment later.

"Maybe it's in your coat pocket," Gregory offered.

James stared indulgently at Gregory. "I'm not stupid enough to stuff pieces of paper with important tel numbers on them in my…" He pulled out the paper. "Get me a tel."

"Pick one out yourself!" Gregory said indignantly.

James sneered at him and got out of the car to get in the sack in the backseat. He chose a tel at random, dialed and let it ring, listening carefully to the recorded message before he was satisfied that no one was in the building to answer. He tossed the tel back in the sack and closed the door. He reached for the handle of the driver's door and was surprised to see Gregory sitting in the driver's seat.

"Everything all right?" Gregory asked.

James walked around and got in the passenger's side, folding the paper with the number on it to put into his wallet. "Yeah, everything's fine."

Gregory smiled. "Do we go to Plan B?"

"Yes, Plan B. Let's circle the block to make sure there are no police around, then park in front of the front doors."

Gregory drove them around the block and parked in front of the laboratory. Cautiously, they eased their way up to the massive front doors. James peered into the lobby, looking for any signs of life. At the same time, he pulled a pair of white gloves from his suit pocket and, with a grand flourish, put them on. He turned and whispered to Gregory, which added drama to the moment in the dim light.

"The keys," he said simply.

Gregory also pulled out a pair of white gloves and slipped them on. He then reached into an inside coat pocket and brought out Richard's keycards. Silently, he handed them to James, but James fumbled his hand against Gregory's in the darkness, and the keys fell to the cement steps.

Gregory was quick to apologize. "Sorry!" He bent down to retrieve them.

James repressed his urgent desire to knock Gregory over the head. Instead, he kicked him.

"Be careful, you idiot!"

Gregory howled and started to retaliate, but James shushed him. "Good grief! Do you want to wake the entire block?" James whispered loudly.

Gregory bit his tongue and shook his head.

James bent over and retrieved the keys. "Let's get on with it," he said. He picked out the security card and inserted it in the slot. A green light flashed, and the reader displayed - Please Insert Keycard. James held the keys closely in front of his face, carefully fingering each key with his right hand. Finally, on the fifth key, he smiled. "This is it," he announced. He inserted it and sure enough, another green light and James pulled open the door.

Gregory was, as usual, amazed. "I see it again," he said, "but I still don't believe it. How do you do that?"

"Practice, my boy, practice… and perhaps a certain mental gift."

Quickly, they entered the lobby, making sure the door locked behind them. Once inside, James held up his hand to stop Gregory from blundering across the room. He reached into his coat pocket and pulled out a small vial. The label read "Sodium Tri-Ulfa Francium (STUF)." James turned the lid until it looked like a saltshaker, then he shook a little of the material in front of them. As the chemical floated through the air, the radioactive Francium reflected in a narrow beam of light.

"Photoelectric eyes," James whispered. "They are overconfident of their technology. That's why they don't have any guards. All I have to do is sprinkle this STUF, obtained at great expense I might add, so we can see the beams."

Carefully, James led them across the lobby, sprinkling STUF continuously to locate the photo-eye beams. They stepped over and ducked under the beams until they reached the elevator.

Gregory shook James by the sleeve. "How do we figure out which floor the Time Lab is on?"

"No problem." James once more held the keys in front of his face and fingered each one. "Floor forty," he announced.

Gregory just shook his head as James inserted the security card again and they entered the elevator. Swiftly they were carried to the fortieth floor. Had they hesitated a moment longer, they may have noticed a dark sedan silently coast up in front of the building and park right behind their car. A large figure got out of it, hurried up to the front door, inserted two keycards and quickly pulled open the door and slipped inside. The figure hesitated but a moment before spotting the photoelectric eye. He moved right to it. A hand flashed in his pocket and came out holding a small device. A quick movement of the device in front of the electric eye, and the entire system deactivated. The figure then waddled over to the elevator.

James flashed his penlight briefly up and down the darkened hallway, although by now, he was convinced that the building was devoid of any security personnel. He had to smile and congratulate himself on his own cleverness in getting past the electronic safeguards. Obtaining the STUF had been an expensive, but wise investment.

More boldly now, James led Gregory down the hall to the clearly marked laboratory of Doctor Elise McAllister. Once again, he held up the set of keys, quickly picked one, inserted it and opened the door. They stepped inside the lab just as the elevator began its descent to the lobby.

The lab was totally dark. James aimed his penlight around the room. They were standing in the anteroom to the actual lab. James moved quietly into the lab, Gregory right on his heels. James moved his light slowly around the room. He was impressed by the array of computers and other sophisticated equipment crammed into the relatively small room. He saw the door that led into Elise's office behind them, and decided immediately that any important materials would obviously be kept locked up in an office. James wished that they could turn on the lights to expedite their search, but there was no use in announcing their movements. He turned to walk to the office and stumbled into a bench across the aisle. He cried out in pain as his shin made direct contact with the metal.

"Damn!"

Gregory, startled by the crash and James' epithet, jumped back in the darkness. He landed up against a rack holding the laboratory coats of Elise, Wende, and Richard. Immediately, his hands shot up. "Don't shoot," he whispered fearfully.

James was hopping about on one foot. "What?" he asked loudly, his voice echoing in the empty room.

Gregory was frightened to the point of whimpering… and he did so now.

James flashed his penlight on Gregory to see what the mumbling fool was carrying on about. He saw Gregory tangled up in a mass of coat sleeves.

"Shut up, you idiot! There's no one there."

Gregory stopped struggling. "Help me up."

James switched off his light. "Get over here. We don't have all night. It's my guess that any computer card is in the office, over there." He pointed in the darkness to Elise's office.

Gingerly, they felt their way to Elise's desk. They left the door open in case they needed to make a quick get-away. James flashed on his light one more time to search for a safe or vault of any kind. He found it on the floor, next to the file cabinet. He turned off the light.

"I must have total concentration, which means I must have complete silence."

Gregory nodded in the darkness.

James waited for an acknowledgement. "Do you understand?"

Gregory nodded once more.

"Gregory!"

"You told me to be quiet!"

James sighed and reached for the combination dial. His sensitive fingertips slowly turned the dial, stopping when he felt the tumblers move inside. He had just gotten the second number when Gregory broke the silence.

"James, I think I hear…"

"Shut up!" James' whisper exploded. "I've almost got it."

"But I think…"

"Shut!"

Gregory sat on the desk with a pout.

James continued his work, and quickly opened the vault. Reaching inside, he snapped on his light. It would help if he knew exactly what he was looking for. He wasn't stupid enough to think that the time machine plans were going to be a large set of blueprints or anything like that. Most likely he was looking for a set of memory cards. He picked up several envelopes, glanced inside them, then cast them aside. He heard a thump and a cry from the other room. He snapped off his light.

"Gregory?"

Silence.

"Gregory!" he hissed louder.

"You told me to shut."

The nearness of Gregory's voice caused James to jump. If Gregory was here, who made the noise in the other room?

"There's someone in the other room," James whispered.

"I know," Gregory nodded. "I tried to tell you, but you told me to…"

"Shush!"

"Well, you said shut up, but…"

James put his hand over Gregory's mouth to quiet him. They listened intently.

Something squeaked in the other room, near the door.

James did what any red-blooded man in this position would do. He picked up a heavy object from the desk and threw it mightily towards the doorway.

There was a yelp of pain when the object made contact.

"Run!" James yelled.

Gregory needed no further encouragement.

They ran over the intruder, out of the lab, and to the elevator. On the main floor, James ran for the front door, scattering STUF wildly about him, not even noticing that there were no beams illuminated because the system had been shut off.

Gregory was pushing him all the way.

Upstairs, the intruder got up groggily, and switched on his own penlight. He entered Elise's office and went directly to the floor vault. It was open and someone had obviously rifled through it. Surprisingly, he located the string box and carefully opened it. It was empty! Whoever had been in here had obviously taken the contents. He retreated, cursing under his breath.

Downstairs, he reactivated the security system. Everything had been spoiled, and the big man was angry. He made sure the front doors were locked behind him, then went to his car, stuffed himself behind the steering wheel, and screeched off into the darkness.

CHAPTER 8

Richard had insisted on spending the night at Elise's apartment again. Elise knew it wasn't necessary and tried to reassure him, but nothing would convince him. The captain had slept most of the afternoon yesterday, so Richard hadn't had much of a chance to talk to him. Elise was relieved at that. She didn't want Richard telling Chris too much. Chris still hadn't asked the fate of his old comrades, and she wanted to handle the question carefully when the time came.

Richard had left for a short while during the evening to go to his own apartment to water his plants and get his pajamas and toothbrush. When he returned, they all retired for the night.

Chris woke everybody up early. Richard growled and complained, but Elise made him get up. She had decided to go to the lab this morning and leave Richard with Chris. She went into the kitchen to fix breakfast for them all while Richard got dressed. Chris went in to take a shower now that he had the controls all figured out so that shower and tub water was comfortable and not scalding. Chris allowed that a fellow could bathe every day and not get tired of it. He seemed to be adjusting quickly.

Elise had just put cinnamon rolls into the oven when the doorbell rang.

Richard looked at Elise. "Are you expecting anyone?"

"No, unless it's Wende." She crossed to the front door. "She probably wants to take another look at Chris." She opened the door.

"Doctor McAllister?" The speaker was an extremely heavy-set man, fifty-ish, and balding, with a large band-aid on his forehead. He was tightly contained in a dark suit. Elise was taken aback at the size of him.

"Yes?"

The stranger stepped into the living room, brushing Elise aside. "May I come in? My name is Lou Ahn." There were two police officers with him, and they followed him inside. Richard was startled. "Louann? What kind of name is that?"

The intruder glared at Richard. "It's not a name. It's two names. A first and a last. Lou Ahn. And you, I presume are Richard Graham?"

Richard looked puzzled. "Yes, I am, but..."

"Then I've come to see you," Lou Ahn said, settling himself onto the couch.

Elise closed the door and moved over to Richard's side. "Who are you, Mr. Ahn?" she demanded.

Lou Ahn held out a card. Elise looked at Richard as she took it and scanned it. Lou Ahn – Private Detective. There was an address and a tel number. She handed it to Richard. He looked at it curiously. "I'm afraid I don't understand," he said. "I'm not looking for a private detective. What do you want? And how did you even know I was here?"

Lou Ahn stretched his arms out across the back of the couch. "I looked for you at your apartment first, but you, obviously, weren't there. It really didn't take a great deal of detective work to guess that you might be over here. I had to come here to question Dr. McAllister anyway. I'm rather glad you're here. It will save us a lot of time and trouble that might have been wasted chasing you down."

"Chasing me down?"

Elise put her hands to her hips. "Now look here, Mr. Lou Ahn. I don't appreciate you busting in here like you owned the place, and I still don't know just what it is that you want. What do you want?"

"And I don't understand why you think that I want a private detective," Richard said, "but believe me, I don't need one now, or any other time, thank you very much."

Lou Ahn laughed a deep rumbling laugh but made no move to get up. Nor did the police officers look like they were going anywhere. "No, you sure don't need a private detective," Lou Ahn laughed. Then his face turned serious. "What you need right now is a real good lawyer."

Richard was completely confused, and Elise was getting angrier by the minute. "If you don't mind," she said, "we really don't have time for any games this morning. We both have work to do at our office, so if you would kindly state your business, then leave."

Lou Ahn rubbed his eyes with an immense back hand. "You're right, Doctor. I don't really have time for games myself. I'm tired. Been up all night, actually. Doctor, a minute ago you mentioned your office, General Amalgamated Laboratories. May I ask what time you left the laboratory last night, and who locked up after you?" His eyes were hard now.

Elise was surprised. "I left fairly early, maybe six or so. My assistant, Wende Merrill, stayed late doing some work. I suppose she locked up when she left."

"What time was that?"

"I have no idea."

"Does she have a complete set of keys? To everything in the laboratory?"

Elise suddenly decided to play her cards close to her vest. "No, only Doctor Bruce and I have a complete set of all keys."

Richard looked at her.

"You're sure? No one else has keys to everything?" Lou Ahn asked, looking directly at Richard.

Richard's face fell. "I have a complete set," he said, embarrassed, "but I don't see what this has to do with..."

Lou Ahn turned his full attention to Richard and cut him

off. "I thought you might remember. Where were you last night?"

"None of your business!" Richard snapped.

Elise spoke up. "He was here, with me."

"All night?"

She flushed. "All night."

"At no time did you leave this apartment?"

Richard thought for a moment. "I left for maybe a half hour or so."

Lou Ahn's eyes narrowed. "And where did you go?"

"To my apartment. I got... some of my things."

"What time was that?"

Richard hesitated.

"Early or late?"

"Fairly late, I guess."

Lou Ahn smiled. "And now the part just like out of the movies. Who saw you?"

Richard stopped. "No one saw me," he said quietly.

"Mr. Ahn," Elise began...

"Please, call me Lou."

"What is this all about? Did something happen at the lab?"

Lou Ahn laughed his rumbling laugh again. "Patience, my dear, patience. I think your friend here knows what I'm talking about, and you'll know soon enough. I assume you will corroborate everything said so far?"

"I don't understand, but yes, it's all true."

Lou Ahn gathered himself together and rolled to his feet. "I think you had better get your coat, Richard. You're going for a little ride with these gentlemen."

Richard planted himself firmly. "I'm not going anywhere. I don't even know what you're talking about!"

"I think you know very well," Lou Ahn said narrowly.

"Well, I don't," Elise said exasperated, "so, would you please fill me in? What do you want with Richard?"

Lou Ahn sighed deeply, as if he were getting ready to explain to a child. "Doctor Bruce had occasion to go to the laboratory extremely early this morning. When he arrived, he found the vault open, and a very valuable piece of memory string is missing."

Richard glanced at Elise. She gave an almost imperceptible nod of her head. No one was supposed to know about the memory string. Richard decided to play dumb. "String? What String? What does this have to do with me?" he asked.

"Whoever was in the lab had a complete set of keys to everything. I've also established that the intruder was a man, possibly two men."

"But I don't have my keys," Richard cried out.

Lou Ahn's eyebrows shot up. "How's that?"

"I lost them!"

Elise was stunned. "You lost your set of keys to the lab?" she almost shouted. "I thought you lost your house keys. Why didn't you say something?"

"There was enough going on and I didn't want to worry you more."

They suddenly stopped, aware that Lou Ahn was listening intently.

Elise took a breath. ""You lost your keycards?"

Lou Ahn wasn't impressed. "Very convenient," he said. "That's what we call establishing an alibi." He pulled a sheet of folded papers from his pocket. "I've got a warrant for your arrest. I'd really rather you didn't make a fuss."

Richard shook his head slowly. "This is all a mistake," he said. "I don't understand it, but it's a misunderstanding of some kind." He looked at Lou Ahn. "We may as well go and get this cleared up."

Lou Ahn smiled. "I'm glad you see things my way." He started for the door as the policemen cuffed Richard.

"I'll call Doctor Bruce and see what's going on," Elise promised Richard. "We'll get to the bottom of this." Tears were in her eyes.

Lou Ahn closed the door behind himself as Richard followed the policemen out of the apartment. Elise collapsed on the couch, crying.

Chris found her there when he emerged from the bathroom, clean and refreshed. He hurried to Elise's side.

"What's wrong?"

"Richard's been arrested!" she said through her tears.

Chris was surprised. "What did he do?"

"He didn't do anything, that's the whole point." Elise tried to wipe the tears from her eyes.

Chris pulled out his handkerchief. "Here," he offered. "Now pull yourself together and tell me exactly what happened."

"They think Richard stole some memory string."

Chris looked blankly at her. "Some memory what ?"

"String."

Chris stroked his chin. "Like... string? Is it valuable?"

Elise sighed. "You wouldn't understand."

He reached over and lifted her chin. "There's a whole lot of things I don't understand, but in order to make the best of a bad situation, I've got to learn. And you've got to teach me. After all, you brought me here."

She fell into his arms, needing to be held. "There's so much happening," she said.

Chris was amazed at the softness of her skin, the smell of her hair. This woman doctor was like no other woman he had ever met.

They sat together in each other's arms until Elise calmed down. Being held tightly in Chris' arms seemed to transfer some of his strength to herself. She was aware of Richard's attentions, but never did she feel like this around him. Slowly, she sat back up. "I'm sorry," she said. "I guess I was just lost for a minute."

Chris stared into her dark brown eyes. "Yeah, I know how it is." He smiled.

Elise got up and crossed to the tel. "I've got to call Wende and find out what is going on. ABBI, call Wende" It was answered on the third ring by a sleepy voice. "Hullo?"

"Wende? This is Elise."

Wende opened her eyes and looked at the clock. Seven-fifteen. "Elise, where are you?"

"Wende, listen carefully. Something terrible has happened."

Wende snapped alert, afraid. "Elise, I..."

"Richard has been arrested."

"What?" she cried, almost dropping her pocket tel. "Richard? How?"

"Just a few minutes ago, a private investigator and some policemen came to my apartment. Apparently, Doctor Bruce went to the lab at an outrageously early hour this morning and discovered that the lab has been broken into. Some memory string is missing. What's going on? Why does this detective think that Richard is involved?"

"Richard didn't steal the string!" Wende almost shouted.

A cold bead of sweat lined Elises' brow. "Please tell me that we're not talking about our master memory string!"."

There was a long pause on the other end of the line. Wende bit her lip before speaking. "No, the master memory string is missing."

Elise's brain didn't register what Wende said. "The master memory string?"

"To the capsule's design. It's gone... but Richard had nothing to do with it."

"You know that, and I know that..."

"No, really, he didn't. I know he didn't."

Elise shook her head. "Of course, he didn't, but it's gone and...oh my God! The *master string* is missing?!"

"Elise, I'm coming right over to your apartment. I can't explain over the tel, but I know what happened to the string... sort of."

Elise paused. "What are you talking about?"

"Give me ten minutes to get there... and don't call anyone else yet, okay?"

"Yes... okay," Elise said, puzzled.

Wende hung up the tel with sweaty palms. Richard arrested for her blunder. The sky was falling in. Hurriedly, she threw on some clothes and ran down to her car. How was she ever going to explain that she was responsible for the missing string?

She pulled out into the mainstream of traffic, cursing herself for not being more careful. So consumed with the calamity of the situation, she didn't notice the older model Chevrolet pull in behind her. She drove quickly to Elise's apartment building. As she hurried through the front door of the building, the Chevrolet parked in front.

Elise opened the door on the first ring.

"Wende, come in. What is this all about?"

Wende walked over to the couch and sat down, crying.

Chris came out of the bedroom where he had hidden until the visitor was identified.

Elise sat down next to Wende and put her arm around the sobbing girl. "Wende, it's all right. Richard is innocent. We'll get him out of it somehow."

Wende sobbed even louder. "Get him out of it?" she cried. "I'm the one who got him into it!"

Elise looked at Chris, then back to Wende. "What, exactly, are you saying?" she asked in an almost calm manner.

Wende rubbed her eyes. "I lost the string," she sobbed.

"Lost it?"

Wende nodded slowly.

Elise sat back on the couch. "Now, when you say you 'lost' the card..." She took a deep breath. "When you say you 'lost' the card, what, exactly, do you mean?"

Wende felt terribly embarrassed and ashamed, but she told them the whole story; working late, the fatigue, losing the string, the search, and her plan to return this morning to find it before anyone found out, but she overslept. "I'm sorry, Elise, I should have stayed until I found it, or I should have called you. I've really made a mess of things." She dropped her head dejectedly. "It was probably all my fault that the capsule malfunctioned in the first place."

Elise hugged her. "It's all right. No real harm has been done. We'll go find the string, then call Doctor Bruce, and get Richard out of jail. I suppose our first move is..."

ABBI's voice broke in. "There is someone at the door."

"Oh, now what? I suppose our first move is to answer the door," she continued. "Chris?"

Chris went into the bedroom and closed the door.

Wende rose and crossed to the door. "I'll get it."

Two impeccably dressed men stood outside. "Doctor McAllister?" the taller gentleman asked.

"No, I'm..." Wende started to correct him, but was interrupted.

"My name is Yuri," James bowed deeply, "and this is Julio. We are with the Embassy."

Wende was puzzled. "Embassy? Embassy Hotel?"

"No, not the Embassy Hotel... it's ... okay, it's a more of a cartel than an actual embassy. May we come in?"

She stepped back uncertainly. James boldly entered; Gregory followed like a shadow.

Elise stepped right up to James. "May I help you? My name is..." She was cut off sharply.

"We've come for the plans," he said.

Both women were genuinely puzzled.

"Plans?" Elise said. "I'm afraid I don't have the slightest idea what you're talking about. Who are you?" She looked at James with a momentary flicker of a memory, but with the shock of the moment, and indeed the entire evening, it fled as quickly as it came.

Gregory grabbed her arm and twisted it slightly.

James smiled. "I'm sorry, we have no time for games." He turned to Wende. "Now, Doctor, we have certain commitments, and we simply must have those plans."

"What plans? What makes you think we have any plans?" Elise blurted out.

Plans. This was the second time that Chris had heard them mentioned. Cautiously, he opened the bedroom door. Gregory was still twisting Elise's arm.

"We don't have a lot of time, if you please. The plans — where are they? We know you brought them from the

125

laboratory."

Chris threw open the door. "The lady says she doesn't know what you're talking about, and I think you oughta let go of her arm."

James and Gregory started in amazement at the previously hidden figure addressing them. He had caught them completely by surprise, and in surprise, Gregory released Elise, but recovered quickly and pulled a small caliber pistol from his coat pocket. He leveled the gun at Chris but spoke to Wende.

"Well, well, well," he said. "Looks as if you've got somebody to rescue you, just like the cavalry, in the nick of time."

James took the pistol from Gregory. "Okay, you, over here." He indicated the couch. "Greg... I mean, Julio, check the other rooms."

Gregory moved to do so. Chris walked slowly to the couch and sat down.

"It is unfortunate that we had to directly involve you in this matter, Doctor, but there is a great deal of money at stake. Had you merely left the plans at the lab, all of this unpleasantness could have been avoided."

Wende sighed. "First of all, I am not Doctor McAllister."

James smiled patiently. Gregory re-entered the room.

"I can't find nothin'. We could tear this place apart and never find somethin' that small."

"What we have here," James said, "is a failure to do what I want. Now, to save us a lot of time and trouble, please, where is the card?"

No one spoke. James sighed.

"Maybe a little persuasion is necessary. Julio?"

Gregory hesitated, realized that he was Julio, and reached for Wende. Chris stood up quickly in between them and stared Gregory right in the eyes. "You touch her, and I'll break your arm," he said softly. His mouth was drawn in a thin line and his eyes hardened.

Gregory stared back at Chris' face. He saw an almost savage

wildness that he had never before seen in a man's face.

"James, keep this guy away from me," he said.

James waved the gun in Chris' direction. "All right, hero, sit down! I'm through playing games." He grabbed Wende's wrist. "You're coming with us until you decide to hand over the plans. I don't care if they're on a a memory card or what. I didn't want to play this way, but you've forced me into it."

Gregory quickly slipped past Chris.

"Julio, get the door," James commanded. He backed up towards the door, keeping Wende between himself and Chris. "Please don't do anything foolish, like calling the police or trying to follow us. We have other... uh... agents watching every move you make." He yanked Wende through the door, and slammed it shut.

Elise fell on the couch. Chris ran to the door. Elise's voice stopped him as he reached for the doorknob.

"Where are you going?"

"After them!"

"Chris, they're armed."

He looked back towards Elise realizing he couldn't pursue these men unarmed. He needed his own gun. But even then, he didn't know how many of them there might be. "You're right," he said at last. "Let's go get the sheriff. We'll get a posse together and follow them."

Elise shook her head. "First of all, we don't have a sheriff and posse. Second, they said that we're being watched, and third, they will be lost in the crowd by now."

Chris nodded. "It would be hard to track them. I noticed that your streets are all worn right down to bedrock." He paused for a minute, thinking. "Have you ever seen those fellows before?"

"Never... I don't think. No." Again, a vague memory, but again, it was gone. "I can't believe this is all happening. And why do they think that Wende is me... just because she answered the door?" She was completely confused. "Wait a minute!" she suddenly shouted. "Their names! They called themselves Yuri and Julio."

Chris shook his head. "Phony names. And what did they mean, 'other agents'? Are they talking about Wells Fargo?"

"No, no, agents are like... well, spies from another country."

Chris' eyes narrowed. "Spies?"

"What did you mean just then when you said, 'phony names'?"

"A good military man listens. Both of them slipped in the excitement and called the other by his real name. One is Greg and the other is James." He smiled. "I may be over a hundred years old, but my mind's still sharp."

Elise got up from the couch. "We've got their names, but what good is that going to do us? We can't exactly look up their names in the tel book with only first names. We're going to need some help."

"The sheriff," Chris said firmly.

"We can't for two reasons," Elise said. "First, we don't have a sheriff upholding the law anymore. That's done by the police department. Second, they said that we're being watched. If some police officers showed up here, there's no telling what might happen to Wende. We just can't risk it."

"Well, we can't get her back sittin' here. There must be something we can do, or someone who can help us."

Elise thought for a moment. "Professor Sanford!" She suddenly said excitedly. "He'll know what to do."

Chris was doubtful. The only professors he knew were road show con men selling snake oil and other worthless items. "I don't know," he said. "The stuff those drummers sell doesn't always do what it's supposed to."

"What are you talking about?" Elise looked at him with a cocked head.

Chris frowned. "These professors..."

Elise stopped him. "Are you thinking of something like Professor Smith and his snake oil?"

Chris nodded.

"We don't have them anymore," Elise assured him. "This professor is a very dear friend of mine. He teaches at Poly Tech University. He's enormously respected, and he has contacts all over the city. If anybody can find out who Wende's kidnappers are, he can."

"Sounds like a soothsayer," Chris said.

"To tell the truth, I've often wondered. We can drive over and see him without arousing any suspicion from anybody that might be watching us. And I'm sure he would just love to meet you."

Chris looked at Elise. "What are we waiting for?"

They left the apartment, trying to walk casually, often glancing over their shoulders, trying to spot someone following them. On the drive across town, Chris watched behind them almost constantly, and soon came to the conclusion that there was no one following them. It had been a ruse.

CHAPTER 9

Elise parked in the university parking lot and hurried, with Chris in tow, to Professor Sanford's office. She knocked on his door.

"Come in, come in," boomed a pleasant voice from within. Chris held the door open for Elise. They entered a huge room with walls of books and sunlight filtering in through tall windows.

The professor looked up from his paper laden desk and beamed when he saw her. "My, but I must be getting along in years," he smiled and stood.

"Why, Professor," she said, giving him a big hug, "what makes you say that?"

"Two calls in one week?" He winked at Chris. "You're expecting me to die soon, is that it?"

Elise laughed nervously. "I expect a lot of things from you, Professor, but that's not one of them."

"And who is your gentleman friend?"

Elise brought Chris forward. "I have a tremendous surprise for you, and a huge problem, or two, for myself. Maybe you had better sit down."

Professor Sanford started to protest.

"Believe me, Professor, you'd better be sitting for this one." She waited until he seated himself in his antique oak swivel chair which creaked and groaned as he sat.

"Now what," he said, "is such a big surprise that I can't take it standing up? Does it involve you and this gentleman friend of yours?" He had a gleam in his eye.

Elise smiled as confidently as she could. "Professor Sanford, may I present Chris Garrett. Chris, Professor Sanford." She watched the professor carefully.

Chris stepped forward and offered his hand. Professor Sanford limply shook the powerful hand, muttering. "Garrett... Garrett. Of course, you were asking about Captain Garrett yesterday. I wondered... You're a descendant, then?"

Chris smiled but remained cautious.

Elise put her arm through Chris'. "Let me rephrase that. Professor Sanford, may I present Captain Chris Garrett, U.S. Army."

The professor's face went blank. "I don't understand." He stared at Chris for a moment, then his face sagged, but his eyes lit up. "No. It's not possible... your time capsule... but you said it malfunctioned."

Chris smiled grimly. "It did, and I'm afraid I'm the result."

Professor Sanford's slack jaw hung down as he stared, wide eyed, at the historical figure before him. He tried to speak but could only mutter nonsense syllables.

"I told you that you had better sit down," Elise said.

"Do you realize what you're saying?" he finally managed to spit out. "Why, this man would have to be..." he did some quick mental calculations, "more than one hundred and sixty years old!"

Elise smiled. "No, Professor, he hasn't lived since then. We brought him into the future rather abruptly."

"Rather," Chris agreed.

"Then, the time capsule works." The professor's eyes began to glow.

"Not exactly," Elise said.

"But you said yourself..."

Elise interrupted him. "I said we had a malfunction. Chris is the result. But I can explain all of that later."

"Later? Do you know what you've got here?"

Elise's face turned serious. "Professor, we've come to see you for help. We need to find the identities of two men."

The professor was shocked. "You've got two more from the past? Elise, you'll upset the balance..."

"Professor, calm down. These two men live here in the city, in our time. All we have to go on are their physical descriptions and their first names – James and Greg. It's most urgent that we locate them!"

The old scholar raised one eyebrow. "And you're telling me to calm down? What's the matter? Why the fuss?"

Elise pleaded, "Please, it's a long story, but someone may be in great danger."

"Danger? There's trouble, then?"

Elise nodded.

"With the time capsule?"

"No... sort of... it's about a person in trouble."

"Because of the malfunction?"

"No, it's... Professor, please, we just need to locate these men before something terrible happens."

"I don't understand. Why don't you go to the police?"

"I can't. We were warned."

"Threatened, is more like it," Chris interjected.

Professor Sanford took Elise's hand. "You've been threatened? By these two? But, why?"

Chris tried to explain. "They think Wende is Elise, and they think she has some string...," he stumbled on the phrase.

"They think Wende is Elise? I have no idea what you are saying. Why do they think Wende is you? What is this about string?"

Elise took over. "Memory string, Professor. It's a brand-new technology that hasn't been made public yet. I'm not even supposed to tell you about it. And Wende is my assistant. These two thugs have confused her for me, and they kidnapped her thinking she could get them the memory string plans for the time vehicle. Only, the string has been lost, and Richard was arrested because it's missing..." She broke off, helpless.

The professor fumbled for the tel. "Good heavens! Why didn't you say it was important? Kidnapped! We'll call the police or the F.B.I. or somebody!"

Elise stopped him. "No, we can't call the police. They told us not to. I don't want to do anything that might hurt Wende. Don't you know anybody else that could help us?"

Professor Sanford thought for a moment, then began dialing the tel. "Describe the kidnappers for me."

Elise described James and Gregory as best she could while he waited for an answer on the tel. "And they said that they were Yuri and Julio and they worked for some foreign embassy. I don't know which one."

"Actually, they said they were with some cartel," Chris said, shaking his head because he didn't know what a cartel was either. There was so much he didn't know.

The professor shook his head. The tel rang again, then was answered. "Lou? Milton Sanford. Fine, thanks, and you? Listen, Lou, I need a favor. I need to locate a couple of fellows. Yes, they have some information I need." He winked at Elise. "This is very important, Lou. Can you help? Sure, let's see... apparently, they are both very well-dressed gentlemen. Impeccably dressed. I have two names – James and Greg, although they are using the aliases of Yuri and Julio." There was a pause. "Yes. That's what I said, James and Greg. They may work for some cartel of some kind. Distinguishing accents?" he looked at Elise who shook her head.

"Possibly Brooklyn," she guessed.

The professor relayed that information then went on to give a physical description, height, weight, and so on as passed on by Elise and Chris. "Would you check on that and get back right back to me? Thanks, Lou. And Lou, thanks for not asking any questions. I knew I could count on an old friend. Good-bye." He hung up. "I have no doubts that we'll have our answer within the hour."

Elise hugged the old man. "Oh, Professor, how can we ever

thank you?"

The professor looked at Chris. "Thank me? How about an hour with Captain Garrett and my digital recorder."

Private detective Lou Ahn sat in his musty downtown office, furiously chewing several pieces of gum. The tel call he had just received was most disturbing. Old Professor Sanford wanted information on two men – James and Gregory. What was disturbing was that he knew James and Gregory. He had talked to them just this morning. They had called the cartel office with some information about plans for a time machine.

That was the trouble with these new full disclosure laws. No one could have an unlisted number anymore. Any quack could call, and they always did, with information to sell. Anything for a quick buck.

Being the ranking cartel officer in the city, any calls that were deemed not crank calls during the initial screening were routed directly to him. He had gotten one such call this morning, James'. What had taken his sudden interest was his own involvement with the memory string plans for the Time Travel Vehicle. Only last night he had tried to procure those plans upon Doctor Bruce's assurance that no one would be in the building. But how could these two bumbling idiots even know about the memory string? It was brand new technology.

Obtaining Doctor Bruce's cooperation had been a great help in the time travel race, but something had gone terribly wrong last night. Doctor Bruce wasn't feeding good information anymore, although Lou Ahn was forced to admit that last night had been the first major slipup. The good doctor took all the right steps this morning, calling him to investigate the 'theft' of the memory string. Lou Ahn didn't get a chance then to let Doctor Bruce know that he didn't know who really had gotten the string. It sure wasn't him. Two other men had it. Then came the call from those clowns, James and Gregory about the 'plans'. Obviously, they had the memory string. Lou Ahn had to arrest one of the technicians who worked in the lab to make it look good.

He was going to have to play it very carefully from now on. Pressure was on from the very top of the cartel to get the string. Doctor Bruce thinks it was stolen by the right hands... and now, Professor Sanford calls asking about James and Gregory. It was curious. What was his involvement? Didn't anybody mind their own business, anymore? Now, what?

He reached for his pocket tel and dialed the number that James had left. It was answered on the third ring.

"Hello?" It was James.

Lou Ahn had told him that he needed time to consider purchasing the memory string. What he really needed was just some time to make sure that they were the ones in the building last night, and that they had the string.

"This is agent Double O-X," Lou Ahn said in a breathy voice. "I'll take the merchandise as offered. Listen carefully, this is how we'll make the payment and the drop..."

James interrupted him. "Yes, well, about those plans... I'm afraid there's a bit of a sticky problem right at the moment. Perhaps my call this morning was a bit premature."

"Do you have the string?"

James hesitated... string? "Well, not exactly..."

"What kind of answer is 'not exactly'?"

James bit his lip and looked at Wende. It was all her fault. If she would only talk, they would be making plane reservations for Acapulco right now instead of trying to explain to Double O-X.

Wende stuck her tongue out at James.

"Well, you see, I'm afraid 'not exactly' is the best description I can give you at this time, unfortunately. However, I do expect the situation to change shortly."

What kind of game was this clown playing? Why say he didn't have the plans after saying he did... and Lou Ahn was certain that he did have it. It just didn't make any sense. "I don't play games," Lou Ahn hissed angrily into the receiver. "I want that string and I want it now! Do you understand?"

James didn't like Lou Ahn's tone of voice at all. And again, with the 'string' thing. "Believe me, I want you to have it, but we've run into a bit of a problem, you see."

Lou Ahn's voice turned absolutely cold and flat. "No, I don't see. I don't want excuses. I want that those plans. If you think you're going to hold out for more money…"

"No, no, the amount is fine, it's just that we don't actually have the actual plans in our hands at this very moment." James' voice broke as he spoke. Double O-X's voice sounded quite threatening.

"Can you get them?"

James thought it strange how the man could make a simple question sound so much like an undeniable order. "We are working on it this very moment, I can assure you."

Lou Ahn growled into the receiver again. "Listen and listen good. Don't do anything until you hear from me again. Do you understand that? Don't do anything until you hear from me!" He waited for an uncertain reply, then punched the tel to shut it off. Those idiots didn't even *have* the string. Richard Graham didn't have it… he certainly didn't have the string… so, who had the memory string? Was Doctor Bruce going back on his word? He didn't think so. The professor's curious involvement might hold the key. He rolled back in his chair. The professor certainly could use some investigating, that was for sure. And what better time than now.

James winced when Double O-X slammed down his tel in James' ear. That was decidedly a crude thing to do. And why was he so upset? It was only a matter of time until James had the memory card safely in his hands, ready for delivery. Indeed, Double O-X should be grateful that James had called him and not any of the other cartels listed in the online tel book. He was willing to bet there were lots of cartels with money out there that would be just as interested and would probably pay even more if they knew they were in competition.

"Whatsa matter?" Gregory asked. "You look like you just lost a whole sack full of wallets. If you was thinkin' any harder, you'd burn somethin' up."

James crossed the room to where Wende sat, hands tied. "Doctor McAllister, my contacts are getting most impatient. *I* am getting most impatient. My colleague is getting most impatient..."

Gregory started to break in, "I'm not getting impatient..."

James stopped him with a glare. "We have avoided any unpleasant scenes because we realize that you are a sensible person. However, time is running out. Where are the plans?"

Wende sighed. "I am not Doctor McAllister, and I don't know where the plans are. If I knew where the plans were, I wouldn't have been at Doctor McAllister's for you to kidnap me."

James shook his head. "Doctor, Doctor, why do you persist in playing games? What, do they give you military training – name, rank, and serial number? This is big business being done on an international scale."

Wende raised an eyebrow. "It is?"

"We are talking about very large sums of money exchanging hands... and serious consequences if we don't have complete cooperation."

Wende was intrigued. International scale? Spies and big money? A damsel in distress? She looked James in the eye. "If I did know where the plans were, would you turn me loose?"

James smiled. Progress at last. "When the plans are mine, you are free to walk out of here."

Wende smiled back at him. "I'm not telling."

CHAPTER 10

Professor Sanford and Chris were engaged in a most detailed discussion. The professor was doing most of the talking, bringing Chris up to date on the battle of the Little Big Horn.

"And so, with Major Reno taking your place, the column charged right into the village. How could they know there were nearly five thousand Indians there instead of the expected one thousand?"

"Why didn't our scouts know this?" Chris asked.

The professor shrugged his shoulders. "You had some Indian scouts, right? Anyway, Reno had it pretty bad, but finally managed to retreat across the Little Big Horn River and up to the bluffs. Sometime later, Captain Benteen and his men joined Reno. About five miles away, Colonel Custer was pinned down. He never stood a chance. The men in his column fought valiantly, but every one of them was lost."

There were tears in Chris' eyes. "Every last man?"

Professor Sanford nodded gravely.

"Wasn't there anything that could be done to help them?"

"Some say that Major Reno could have pulled out to help them, but who knows. As it was, Reno and Benteen barely managed to hold on for two more days, that would be the 27th, until General Terry arrived to help them."

Chris sat back in his chair in dismay and closed his eyes.

"Can you imagine all that they went through?"

Elise was close to tears, herself. "Chris, it's all over. It's just history. Pages in books." She wished she could ease his suffering.

Chris looked at her, his eyes red. "It's not just some pages," he said. "These are living, breathing human beings. I know... knew, these men. I've lived with them, ate with them, laughed with them and cried with them." His voice cracked and he stopped.

"Chris, don't." Tears filled Elise's eyes as she watched him torment himself.

The tel rang at that moment, and the professor answered. Lou Ahn was on the line. "Oh, hello, Lou. Have you got anything for me?"

"Yeah, Milt, I think I've got what you want."

"Great! And so fast, too. It's Lou," he told Elise and Chris as he waved the tel towards them before putting it back up to his ear. "What have you got?" He grabbed a pencil and searched his desktop for a blank piece of paper.

"Milt, I was just kind of curious... these two guys are a couple of small-time crooks... you're not involved with them, are you?"

The professor laughed. "No, not me. Actually, some friends of mine need the information because... I... er... I mean, I'm not sure why."

Lou Ahn frowned. "Forgive me, Milt. I'm not trying to pry."

"That's okay, Lou."

Elise leaned over to Chris. "Lou... that reminds of that Lou Ahn and Richard."

The professor looked over at Elise. "Why, that's amazing. This is Lou Ahn."

Elise was so startled her body jerked. "The detective, Lou Ahn?"

Professor Sanford nodded.

"We met him this morning," she said with alarm. "He's the

one who had Richard arrested."

"What a coincidence," the professor told Lou Ahn. "My friends say that they met you this morning. Under some rather trying circumstances, I'm afraid. Doctor Elise McAllister and Captain... er, Chris Garrett."

Lou Ahn's mouth hung open. "Doctor McAllister?"

"Yes, you remember?"

"Sure, sure. Listen, here's the info you needed." He gave the professor a phony address across town. "That's the last I got on them, anyway."

The professor carefully copied down the address and said, "Thanks, Lou. If I can pay you back in any way, just ask, okay? Good-bye." He hung up. "Well, we've located your men."

Lou Ahn slumped forward (or at least as far forward as someone his size can slump) deep in thought. The pieces of the puzzle were beginning to fall in place. Doctor McAllister had stolen the memory string plans for the time travel vehicle from General Amalgamated Laboratories. But why? It didn't add up... and if she had the string, why did she let him arrest her assistant? Somehow, those two clowns, James and Gregory, were involved, too. What a puzzle. He knew that they were the ones who had bungled his job last night, and for that, they must pay. It was time for another tel call.

James answered on the first ring. "Hello?"

"Double O-X."

"Ah," James acknowledged, "Double Ox. James, here."

"I know who you are, and I'm not double ox... I'm Double O-X. Oh-Oh-X."

"Right. What do you have for me?" James asked authoritatively.

Lou Ahn silently counted to ten. "Do you have the string yet?"

"Ah, yes, that. Not exactly. She's a stubborn girl." James looked over at Wende with agitation. She stared defiantly back into his eyes.

Lou Ahn paused, puzzled. "Who is a stubborn girl?"

"Doctor Elise McAllister," James announced triumphantly. "We have her in our possession. She's insisting she isn't who she is, but of course, she is. She also says she doesn't have the plans, but we know better."

Lou Ahn slapped his forehead with his open palm. "You idiot!" he screamed, "she hasn't got the plans!"

There was a pause. "That's what she says."

"And she is not Doctor McAllister!"

A longer pause... then, "That's... that's what she says, too."

"The real Doctor McAllister has the string. She and somebody named Garrett." Lou Ahn thought for a moment. "Captain Chris Garrett."

James nodded. "That must be the guy in the apartment this morning."

Lou Ahn's voice hardened. "Get that string!"

"It's practically in your hands," James assured him.

Lou Ahn mashed his pocket tel in his massive hands.

James turned to Gregory. "We're wasting our time with her. She hasn't got the card... or string something or other. She's not even who she says she is."

Gregory was surprised. "She isn't?"

"I never said I was Doctor McAllister," Wende said. "I'm Wende Merrill."

"And you're not going to tell us where the card is, are you?"

Wende drew her lips into a thin line.

"Shall I beat it outta her?" Gregory asked.

James smiled confidently. "No need for that. We know who has the card."

"We do?"

Wende's eyebrows went up. "We do?"

"I believe the real Doctor McAllister knows where the memory card is." James said. He watched Wende's face for a reaction. "I also believe your friend, Garrett, knows. Captain

Garrett."

She gasped. "No one knows about him yet!"

James' smile widened with this discovery. A soft spot. "I have my sources," he said, nodding towards a tel on the table.

Gregory spoke up. "Hey, that's the guy in the apartment this morning."

Wende smiled. "He can't help you. He doesn't even know what memory string is. They didn't exactly have them in his day."

James scratched his chin. "His day?"

"1876," she said. "That's when the capsule malfunctioned."

Gregory shook his head questioningly. "What is she talking…?"

James frantically motioned for him to shut up. "Go ahead," he said.

"You already seem to know it all."

"Ah, yes, but you could fill in the details." James was trying to put the pieces together, but he was struggling. So far, he could make no sense of what Wende was saying.

"None of us know the details," Wende admitted. "We may never know what caused Captain Garrett to be brought into the future. Poor man. That wasn't supposed to happen."

"The future!" Gregory shouted. "You mean, he's…"

James glared at Gregory with a stern, silent 'shut up!' He turned back to Wende. "Of course," he said calmly, although he was really stunned. "Captain Garrett was in the army in 1876."

Wende laughed. "At least we saved him from being killed along with everyone else."

James nodded. "Yes, being killed." He watched Wende to see if she would go on.

"How could he know that Custer's whole column would be wiped out?"

Custer! James was absolutely amazed. It wasn't possible… and yet, here he was haggling over plans for a time capsule. It *was* possible. More than that, it was an indisputable fact! Captain Garrett was proof, and James had seen him with his own eyes.

He looked at Wende.

"My dear, you are going to get that memory card for us," he said.

Wende was defiant. "I'll do no such thing. And it's not a card, it's..." She stopped as she suddenly realized that these two idiots didn't know about the memory string. They probably hadn't even ever heard of memory string. They think the plans are on an old memory card!

James smiled. "I think you shall. And you will gain your freedom in the process. Gregory, bring me my laptop."

Gregory started across the room, then stopped short. "We don't have a laptop. We pawned the last two we got."

"Is our neighbor, Patrick, home?" James asked.

"Nah, he works during the day."

"Then we can use his computer."

"But his door is locked," Gregory protested.

James gave Gregory a fatherly look. "Has that ever stopped you before?"

Gregory grinned. "You're right. I've got my tools in my wallet."

Wende was curious despite her precarious situation. "What are you going to do?"

"A little masquerade, my dear," James told her. "You see, we could simply trade your life for the memory card, but doesn't that sound crude? It simply lacks class. I mean, everybody does that sort of thing, don't they?"

Wende sniffed. "I would hardly know."

"Well, take my word for it." James stood and paced, obviously enjoying himself. "I would like to think that I am above simplicity. Look at Gregory. Gregory is a paragon of simplicity."

Gregory blushed. "Aw, go on."

James shook his head solemnly. "No, I mean it... but I'm getting away from my story. As I was saying, I like to feel that I am a master of my craft."

"As a kidnapper?" Wende spat out.

James laughed. "Not at all. This is but a sideline. I like to think that I am a master of deception."

Wende eyed him closely, as did Gregory. "I don't understand."

"I am going to meet with Captain Garrett. Actually, that's a fallacy."

"It is?" Gregory said, surprised.

"Captain Garrett is going to meet with his commanding officer, General George Armstrong Custer. Being a good soldier and officer, as I have no doubts he is, Captain Garrett will willingly comply with General Custer's orders to turn over that memory card."

Gregory shrugged. "Why can't I think of these things?" He looked at James in admiration.

"Once we have the memory card safely in our hands, we'll have no further use for you, Miss Merrill, and you may go free." He smiled and rubbed his hands together gleefully.

Wende surprised herself and said, "But you said that you were going to use me!"

James shrugged and sat down. "Only if Captain Garrett refuses to obey a direct order from a commanding officer. But I don't think that will happen. Gregory, if you don't mind..."

Gregory stared at him.

"The computer. Lead the way, please."

"Oh, yeah." Gregory jumped up and led the way out the door.

James helped Wende to her feet and prodded her forward.

"I can wait here," she said.

James pushed her in the back. They all went two doors down past Thelma's apartment. Thelma didn't have a computer anymore.

Gregory had little trouble with the door lock. He didn't have the touch that James did, but he wasn't totally inexperienced, either.

Once inside, James immediately went to the computer and turned it on. He quickly brought up the Internet and typed in a

Google search command. "Here we are," he said, "George Armstrong Custer. Good description of the battle of the Little Big Horn, and more importantly, a good picture of the man."

"I still don't understand," Wende said.

Gregory laughed. "It's simple."

Wende looked at him in confusion.

Gregory smiled. The smile faded. He shook his head and looked at James. "Okay, I got nothin'. I don't get it either."

"I'm sure I can rustle up a decent costume," James said, "with a blond wig. And with a minor amount of studying the details, I shall become the illustrious General Custer."

Gregory smiled again and pointed at James as if to say, 'told you so'.

Wende shook her head in disbelief.

Chapter 11

Elise was elated. They had an address where they would undoubtedly find James and Greg... and Wende. After a hurried discussion, she and Chris had decided to try and rescue Wende themselves. The fewer people involved, the better. Elise was sure by now that Chris could do it if he put his mind to it. He was an amazingly resilient and resourceful man. They had thanked the professor profusely, got in Elise's car, and driven to the cross-town address. Ten minutes after leaving the professor's office, they were out into the industrial district, cruising back and forth in front of a relatively large warehouse.

"Are you sure you followed the directions right?" Chris asked. "I mean, there are so many streets, we might have just slipped by the right one."

Elise shook her head. "This is right. At least, it's what Professor Sanford wrote down for us. Maybe they're inside someplace."

"Those hombres were pretty duded up to be holed up in a place like this."

"What did you expect?"

Chris looked over the weather worn metal building. "Me? Expect? Boy, I'll believe just about anything now, but I don't *expect* anything."

Elise stopped the car. "Well, I don't know any other way to find out whether or not they're in there, except to go in and look... unless you've got some modern way to see through walls," Chris at length.

"Actually, there are... but we don't have any of that equipment," Elise smiled thinly.

Chris got out of the car and took off his jacket. "Wait here."

He walked boldly up to the front door. It was locked. The lack of any windows in front didn't particularly impress him since windows (especially glass ones) were somewhat of a luxury in the 1876 Montana Territory.

He circled the building, trying two more doors in back. They were locked also. There was a large, corrugated metal door at one end of the building, but Chris didn't even recognize it as being a door. There was a small rectangular window over each of the regular doors in back of the warehouse. One of the windows was mostly shattered out. Chris stood under it. He could probably jump up and grab the sill, it was only seven feet or so high, but he would surely cut his hands on the broken glass.

The sides of the metal building absorbed and radiated heat from the high summer sun, bathing Chris in perspiration.

Along the side door were two metal containers that looked to Chris to be barrels made of metal. He pushed one and yanked his hand back. The metal was hot. He kicked them to see if they were empty. The return hollow sound told him that they were. He pushed one with his feet until it was directly under the window. He hesitated, trying to figure a way to get up on the barrel without burning his hands. There was a handkerchief in his back pocket that he wrapped around his right hand. He was going to have to grin and bear it as far as his other hand. He took a step back, and with his covered hand, vaulted precariously up on the barrel.

There were shards of glass all over the sill that Chris carefully picked up and tossed on the ground. With the handkerchief still on his hand, he knocked out the remaining glass in the window.

There was something, he couldn't quite put his finger on it, that made him hesitate. A low hum inside the building caught his attention, but something else... the air streaming out the window was not hot. It wasn't really cool air, either. It was just sort of neutral, but it was moving. This building must have... what did Elise call it?... climate control. He put his head on the windowsill and leaned in to look and listen. The only sound was that of the climate control unit. He could see that the door below him led into some sort of small room, like an office. There was a desk, chair, and file cabinets.

Chris pulled himself up and through the window. The only light in the office was from the window he had just entered. Chris spotted a light switch, but quickly decided against using it. The element of surprise was worth too much. He carefully crossed the office to another door which, he surmised, led into the rest of the building. It did. He was now in a cavernous room, apparently a storeroom of some sort, larger than any storeroom he had ever seen. It was very dark as the only light came in from another high window at the opposite end of the room...and a thick layer of dust coated everything! There were rows and rows of some kind of long hollow tubes – like clay pipe that he had seen used in the cities back east - all neatly stacked and covered with this infernal clay dust from the pipe itself.

Chris had to wait for his eyes to adjust to the dim light before he started exploring, but already he had decided that it was very unlikely anyone was holed up here.

Overhead were several low hanging canvas tubes that pulsed to the rhythm of the climate control motor. Even as he watched and listened, the unit cycled off, the tubes relaxing. Chris reckoned that he could reach up and touch those tubes if he stood on top of one of the stacks of pipe. He also couldn't fathom how things turned themselves on and off in this city. He just shook his head.

It was apparent that the dust had been settled for some time, and the total lack of footprints soon assured him that no one was in the building but himself. He was disappointed, even though he couldn't really see how this whole affair was any of his business. He had enough troubles of his own. Although, he couldn't put up with the thought of kidnappers... and besides, Elise had helped him.

He left the building the same way he had entered and returned to the car.

"Look at you!" Elise cried. "You're a mess."

"Yeah, I reckon you're right." He started brushing himself off. "What kind of place is this, anyway?"

"Looks like it's a storage warehouse for clay pipe," she told him. "They manufacture it next door and apparently store it here."

"What's it for?"

Elise looked puzzled. "I don't know... water and sewer lines I guess."

Chris finished brushing himself off the best that he could. "There aren't any footprints but my own in there. That place has been deserted for a while."

Elise was thinking. "Maybe Professor Sanford got the address wrong. Maybe he meant the manufacturing plant next door instead."

"Maybe he did," Chris said. "But maybe he meant any of these buildings. It would take a long while to search them all, and we'd be bound to be seen going in and out of all of them."

Elise's shoulders slumped. "You're right. So, now what do we do?"

"We wait. That's all we can do. We wait for them to contact us."

"But when might that be?"

"Your guess is every bit as good as mine."

They were back to nowhere in no time.

Chapter 12

"I certainly hope they call soon." Elise was fixing a snack for Chris and herself. She had called Professor Sanford as soon as they had returned to the apartment and told him of their wild goose chase. He had promised to call Lou Ahn again.

"All we can do is wait," Chris said.

"I hope they didn't try to call while we were out." Sudden alarm crossed her face. "Oh, Chris! What if we've missed them?" She asked ABBI for any messages. There were several, but not from the kidnappers.

"Calm down. They'll call any minute." He was nervous, too.

An hour later, their sandwiches untouched, ABBI announced, "Incoming call for Elise."

"Put it on speaker," Elise said excitedly. "Hello!"

A man's voice boomed out in the air. "Doctor McAllister? This is Julio." It was Gregory.

Chris looked around to see who was speaking, but he and Elise were the only ones in the room.

"Yes, this is Doctor McAllister. Where are you? Is Wende all right?" The questions tumbled out.

"Is Captain Chris Garrett with you?"

Elise paused. Captain Garrett? How did they know his full name... and more importantly, his rank?

She was cautious. "Yes, he's here."

"Put him on."

She frowned. "They want to talk to you.," she whispered.

Chris stood, looking confused.

"Captain Garrett? Are you there?"

Chris' eyes widened as he heard the voice speak his name.

Elise whispered again, "Say something."

"Captain?"

"Yes… I'm…" Chris broke off in amazement at the sound of Gregory's voice coming out of the air. He wasn't sure where to look.

Gregory took on an authoritative tone. "Captain Garrett, stand by for General George A. Custer."

Chris blinked. General Custer? It couldn't be. Custer was a Lieutenant Colonel.

"Did I hear that right?" Elise whispered in the background."

"It's Colonel Custer," he whispered.

Elise looked puzzled.

An odd sounding voice suddenly boomed through the air. "Captain Garrett?"

Whoever it was, it certainly wasn't the Colonel. "Yes," he said cautiously.

"Captain, this is your commanding officer, General George A. Custer. How are you, my boy?" James had practiced all day on a reasonable sounding (or so he thought) gruff voice. Gregory had certainly been impressed. "It's good to talk to you again."

Chris was amused even through the seriousness of the situation. Colonel Custer was not about to refer to one of his officers as 'My Boy.' "I'm fine sir, how's the missus?"

James wasn't prepared for that question. "Quick," he called to Gregory, "what was Custer's wife's name?"

Gregory's shoulders slumped and his mouth dropped open.

Wende immediately realized from that one question Captain Garrett knew of the hoax and grinned as she looked upward.

James shook his head at Gregory's ignorance. "Ah, she's fine, Captain, just fine. Listen, what I called about was…"

Chris interrupted him. "Colonel... I mean General, you don't know how good it is to hear your voice. I have been extremely worried about you... the battle and all."

Pause.

"The battle. Yes. The battle of the Little Big Horn. Terrible thing. Very messy. All those Indians and all."

Chris nearly laughed but held himself in check in view of the seriousness of the situation and the reminder of his compadres' fate. "Well, it's certainly comforting to know that you made it through all right, sir. Now, what can I do for you?"

James cleared his throat. "I need to meet with you, Captain."

Chris was surprised. "A meeting, sir?"

"Yes. It has come to my attention that a friend of yours, a Doctor McAllister, has a small computer memory card. A very valuable card, I might add. I'd like to get my hands... I mean, I'd like to see it. The President may be interested in it, my boy."

"The President."

"Yes, President..." a look of panic crossed James' face as he realized that he had no idea who the president of the United States was in 1876. "Um... *The* President," he sputtered.

Elise couldn't stand it. "Is he kidding?" she whispered.

James continued. "I could order you to bring it to me, Captain, but I thought I'd ask, one officer to another, you know."

Chris motioned to Elise to be quiet while he thought. "Yes sir, I appreciate how you feel. Where would you like to meet?"

"I think we should meet on neutral ground."

Wheels turned in Chris' mind. "There's a warehouse across town," he gave the address that they had gotten from Lou Ahn, "are you familiar with it?"

James and Gregory were familiar with every possible hideout in the city. "Yes, Captain, I know the place." James smiled. Perfect. No witnesses there. "Shall we say eight o'clock tomorrow morning?"

"That would be fine, General... and General? There's one

more thing. Another friend of mine, a Miss Merrill, is missing. I'm very worried about her. Could you look into it for me, sir?"

"Of course, my boy. I'll have her released as soon as the memory card is in my hands... I mean... I'll certainly look into it, Captain. Until tomorrow, then." James saluted into his tel and hung up.

ABBI ended the call and Chris chuckled.

"I don't believe it," Elise said in amazement.

Chris looked at her. "Don't be fooled," he said, "that was James and Greg. One of them is pretending to be General Custer, and he has asked me as 'one officer to another' to turn over the memory card." He sat down.

Elise cocked her head at him. "Yeah, I kind of got that."

"They'll let Wende go in exchange for some kind of card... a memory card?"

Elise's head was starting to pound from tension and worry. "I think they mean the string, but we don't have it."

"They think we do."

"What are we going to do?"

"Calm down and do some thinking."

Elise got up and started pacing back and forth in front of the couch. "Boy, I'd like to get my hands on those two," she said, as she balled her hands into fists so tight the knuckles of her hands were white. "We're running out of time. Doctor Bruce is going to be down all our throats soon if I don't get him a report of some kind. How am I ever going to explain the lost memory string... or you?" She made a show of giving up trying to think about it.

Chris grabbed her hands. "You know, before, all I could think of was getting home. Now, I'm not so sure. It's like I'm supposed to stay." He got up and started pacing, himself. "We've got to come up with a plan."

"Such as?"

"Divide and conquer... deception... I don't know 'such as'. It would be nice to if we could play their little game with them."

Elise sniffed. "Who are you going to pretend to be? The

president?"

"No," Chris said, "I don't pretend to be anybody... by the way, who is president?"

"Sheryl Stockton."

Chris' eyes widened. "A woman?"

Elise smiled and nodded.

"Anyway, we give them a different memory string," he said, shaking his head.

Elise thought for a moment. "Do you think they're stupid enough to fall for it?"

Chris looked back at her. "One of them is pretending to be General Custer and expecting me to believe it, and you ask if they are stupid enough to fall for it?"

"Except, how do we get another memory string? They're not your everyday garden variety of string, you know."

"No, I don't know. I don't even know what one looks like. What is it? Is it smaller than a saddle blanket?"

"A memory string is a way of storing data by creating magnetic impulses in a helix and... wait..." She got up and crossed to her closet, rummaging through a box before finding what she was looking for. She tossed him a piece of gold decorating string."

"What's this?"

"That's just some Christmas decoration stuff, but it looks sort of like memory string. Memory string is gold, like that and about that size in diameter."

Chris blinked.

Elise laughed. " Memory string is like a piece of this She stopped and snapped her fingers. "Of course, I've got it! We'll just substitute a piece of this for the memory string. They're not going to know the difference! It might fool these guys in a dark room." Then she stopped.

"What is it?" Chris saw the look on her face.

"They kept referring to the plans being on a memory card. Maybe they didn't mean string. Maybe they don't know about the string." She went to her desk and rummaged through a drawer, finding a memory card. "This is a memory card. We can give them this and tell them it has the plans on it. They'll never know the difference! Especially if we're in a dark room!"

"I'm gonna gamble that they'll want to keep the lights off," Chris mused, "to keep me from getting a good look at 'General Custer'. In fact, I'll see to it that we talk in the far end of the warehouse. There weren't any windows on that end, so it will be fairly dark... dark enough, anyway."

They were startled at that moment by the buzzing of the doorbell. Chris and Elise looked at each other with concern. More bad news? Elise opened the door.

"Hi. Remember me?"

"Richard!" Elise hugged him. "How did you get here? How did you get out of jail?"

Richard crossed to the couch and wearily sat down. "Well," he began, "Lou Ahn took me straight to the precinct and had me booked. What an experience that is. I've still got ink on my hands from the fingerprinting. Anyway, I was allowed one tel call, so I called you, figuring you'd get this cleared up right away, but no one answered, so I didn't bother to leave a message."

Elise's eyes widened. "Oh, Richard, I'm so sorry. We were gone."

"I gathered as much. I don't know any lawyers, so I just sat there. Then, about a half hour ago, Lou Ahn showed up and got me out. He said it was a mistake. I don't like that man. There's something... well, sinister about him."

Chris cleared his throat and Elise looked away.

"Richard, something important has happened."

Richard nodded. "Oh, sure, something real important, right?"

Elise looked at him. "Wende has been kidnapped."

"What?!" His eyes searched Elise's face.

"Not long after you were arrested. Wende came here to tell me that while working late at the lab, she lost the master memory string."

"I don't understand. Wait... what do you mean 'lost' the

memory string? Where is she?"

Chris took up the story. "While she was here, two small time crooks showed up pretending to be some kind of spies, and wanting a memory card from Wende, who they thought was Elise."

"Spies?"

"When we didn't... couldn't... turn it over, they took Wende."

They wanted a card? What card?"

"We think they mean the string."

"Where?"

"We don't know where."

"Did you call the police?"

Chris shook his head. "They warned us not to call the sheriff. We talked to..." Chris waved his hand for help.

"Professor Sanford," Elise offered.

"And he called Lou Ahn for help."

Richard did a double take. "Lou Ahn?"

"He gave us an address where he thought they might be, but no one was there." Chris sat down next to Richard. "We came back here to wait for a call, and we got it just a few minutes ago."

"You've talked to Wende, then? Is she all right?"

"We didn't talk to her, but I'm certain that she's okay. James and Greg have figured out that she isn't Elise, and now they want to trade her for the memory card. I'm meeting with them in the morning to make the exchange."

"Then you have the string?" Richard asked.

"No, they don't know about the string. They think the plans are on a memory card, so we're going to give them this." She held up the card.

Richard's eyes narrowed.

Elise helped him. "It's just a memory card out of my desk drawer. We think this will fool these guys in the right light."

"How do you know that they'll turn her over?" Richard asked at length. "What guarantee do you have?"

"It's a gamble that we have to take," Chris said.

"A gamble? This isn't 1876, Captain. It's 2045 and we don't gamble with people's lives."

Elise gently touched Richard's arm. "Richard, calm down. We have absolutely no reason to suspect that they'll harm Wende. There have been no threats, and from what we know of these two, they're just small-time crooks. I'm not sure how they got involved, but kidnapping doesn't seem to be their forte."

Richard turned to Chris. "You called them by name. Do you know who they are?"

"We only know what Lou Ahn told us, "Chris said.

Richard wasn't convinced and it irritated him that Elise was letting herself be swayed by a man a hundred and fifty-five years behind the times. He clenched his jaw and eyed Chris. "What's your plan of attack?"

Plan of attack? Chris suddenly flashed back to the events of only a couple of days ago... or was it longer? Attack? No, they mustn't attack. "My plan is to meet with them as they asked and take it from there."

"I'm going with you."

Chris shook his head. "I'm meeting with Colonel Custer."

Richard raised an eyebrow. "You're meeting with...Colonel Custer?" He looked at Elise in disbelief. "Elise, we don't know all the side effects of time travel. We don't know *any* of the side effects of time travel. The strains, tensions..."

Elise smiled and shook her head. "One of those crazy crooks is going to dress up like Colonel Custer, only they think he was a general, and try to fool Chris. He's already tried to fool him over the tel."

"I need my sword belt," Chris said. "And I'd feel better if I was armed with my pistol."

"You're expecting trouble?" Richard asked.

"If there's one thing I've learned," Chris replied, meeting Richard's gaze, "It's to expect anything at any time."

"Your belt is still at the lab," Elise said. "Perhaps Richard and I could get it. We've got to go back and face the music sooner or later anyway."

Richard rose and crossed to a window. He drew the curtain and looked out over the city. Darkness had fallen and thousands of pinpoint lights sparkled below.

"So much, happening so fast. In such a short time our lives have been completely upset. And all since you came here, Captain. That's when all the changes began."

Chris stood up and looked at Richard. "Believe me," he said, "you don't know how a life can change in a short time."

Richard stared at the lights as he sorted things out. "I'm sorry, Captain. I'm just upset. I'm worried about Wende. I'm tired. Elise, why don't we go down to the lab and find out what's been happening."

They took a few minutes getting ready. Elise decided that it was best if Chris did not accompany them, and Chris agreed, allowing as how he was 'a little tired.' Elise asked ABBI to turn on the T.V. to keep Chris company while they were gone. He sat, mesmerized by the figures on the large screen, and didn't even notice when Elise and Richard closed the door behind themselves. He watched until the ten o'clock news began, but fatigue weighed on him until he quietly fell asleep, the T.V. still on. The newscaster droned on about muggings, world tension, and more news from General Amalgamated Laboratories. Although details were sketchy, "apparently the world's first time machine had been tested at least partially successfully. Doctor Bruce, Director of G.A. Labs refused comment about the test, and Doctor Elise McAllister, head of the project, was unavailable for comment. Questions were beginning to be asked due to the lack of information from the project leaders. What actually had gone on? General Amalgamated Labs was surrounded by police and secrecy. No one was allowed to enter the building without special clearance. Stay tuned to W.R.A.P. for further details."

Chapter 13

Elise couldn't have been more surprised by the police stationed all around the building, and every other person seemed to be a reporter. She and Richard were stopped at the door by a burly policeman.

"Where do you think you're going?" he demanded.

Elise was affronted. "What are you doing? What's going on here? We've got to get upstairs."

"Sure, you do. And which newsfeed outlet are you with?"

"We're not with any newsfeed outlet," Richard bristled. "This is Doctor Elise McAllister, and I am Richard Graham. We work here."

The cop stepped back and stared at Elise. A petite, young woman quickly stepped up near them.

"Did I hear you say that you are Doctor Elise McAllister?" she asked.

Elise nodded. "Yes, and I must get upstairs."

"Doctor," the girl began, "my name is Jan Stricker, from station W.R.A.P. Can you tell me what happened with your test?"

"I can't tell you anything." Elise tried to brush past the reporter. "Officer, I've got to get in this building."

The officer smiled. "Don't worry, Doctor McAllister, Officer Mundy will be more than happy to escort you up." He looked to his partner. "Directly to Doctor Bruce on floor forty!"

Elise and Richard were led roughly into the waiting elevator. Their minds were racing. They were at last going to meet Dr. Bruce... and oh, how they now dreaded it!

Jan Stricker tried to follow.

"And where do you think *you're* going?" It was the burly officer.

Jan smiled. "Officer, the scoop of the century is going on inside there, and I'm out here." She softened her face. "Now, if you were to be looking over there," she pointed with a finely manicured finger, "maybe I wouldn't be here bothering you when you looked back." She smiled sweetly.

"Nothin' doin', lady." He crossed his arms defiantly. "Nobody, but nobody, gets up there... Lady?... Lady?..."

Jan smiled to herself once she was inside the door. During the big cop's show of authority, he had closed his eyes for a moment, perhaps hoping she would be gone when he opened them. She was. She glanced at the small group of security officers near the elevator, then strode boldly to the stairway and began her long ascent. It might as well have been Mt. Everest.

Exhaustion and hyperventilation almost overtook her, but finally, painfully, Jan cautiously opened the door to the fortieth floor. The hallway was clear. Without hesitation, she went directly to the door with Doctor McAllister's name over it. She listened for a moment, then slipped inside. Voices drifted in from the inner lab. She glanced around the anteroom looking for a place to hide. The voices suddenly became louder, and Jan decided that now was as good of a time as any to see if the closet was unlocked and big enough to hide in. She had barely closed the door behind her as Elise, Richard, and Doctor Bruce entered the anteroom.

Doctor Bruce was speaking. "Why you didn't come to me with this right away, I'll never know."

"I thought it was best not to let it out until I had the situation under control," Elise stammered. She still couldn't believe that he was here in person.

"Under control? You call the situation 'under control?' I'll tell you, Doctor, the only thing that may... and I emphasize, may... save your job is if you speak up about the man on the video recording. If we have what I think we have..." He broke off in awe.

"What we have is a malfunction," Richard picked up. "We have a time travel machine that doesn't work right."

Doctor Bruce whirled around. "Doesn't work right? What we have is the find of the century! Of all time! A man from the past. Don't you realize what this means to the world? To me?"

Jan almost tumbled out of the closet. A man from the past? That couldn't be right. But is that what all the big hush was about? She pictured herself being handed the Pulitzer Prize for investigative reporting.

Doctor Bruce broke her reverie. "We could take the man on tour. We'd make a fortune. I demand that you tell me where he is!"

"I can't tell you," Elise stammered.

"You will!"

"Doctor Bruce, we can't tell you anything until..."

"Until what?"

"Until we get Wende back safely," Richard burst out.

Doctor Bruce stared at him. "Get Wende who back from where?"

"It's a very long story," Elise said.

"I've got all night."

Elsie sat down and told him how her assistant, Wende Merrill (oh, that Wende!), has stayed late working on the malfunction while Elise and Richard chased the captain. She told of Wende showing up frantic because the memory string had been lost, and of her kidnapping.

"We must find that memory string!" Doctor Bruce thundered. "Lost. I don't believe it! Why aren't you two out looking now?"

Elise and Richard looked at each other in disbelief.

"Because we're talking to you," Richard said.

"Well, for God's sake, man, don't just stand around here. Get out and do something."

Elise needed no more encouragement. She headed straight for the door. Richard took a roundabout route and grabbed Chris' sword and gun belt from a hook by the door. He stuffed them under his lab coat and quickly followed Elise out the door.

Jan listened intently for a moment, then heard the beep-beep of a pocket tel being dialed. A pause, then...

"Double O-X? This is Bruce. Listen, you bungler! I've got to have that string! You've messed this up from the beginning and it's gone on too long. I don't care! There's more to this than you can imagine. McAllister just left the lab. Get down here and follow her until she turns up the string. If I ever get caught in this, you're going down with me!" He slammed the tel with a finger to turn it off and hurried out of the door.

Jan held her breath. She slowly opened the closet door and inched her way out of the lab and down the hallway to the stairs. She took a deep breath and started her descent. She had plenty of time to sort out her thoughts.

A man from the past, a kidnapping, something called a memory string theft investigated by Doctor Bruce and involving someone called Double O-X. Very interesting, indeed. If only she had caught more of the conversation, but the slow climb up forty flights of stairs had nearly killed her. She was glad to have heard what she did. A man from the past would make quite a story.

Elise and Richard pushed their way through the crowding group of police and reporters outside the building. Elise was amazed at the tenacity of the reporters. It was nearly midnight, but she supposed that they weren't about to give up and leave until there was no one left in the building. What reporters wouldn't do for a story. She was surprised that none of them had tried to sneak into the lab.

They drove straight to Elise's apartment and found Chris sound asleep on the couch. Richard took one look at him and decided to leave him right where he was.

"He's sleeping, he looks comfy, and I seem to remember getting laughed at the last time I tried to pick him up."

Elise pulled off Chris' shoes. "I guess he'll be all right until morning."

Richard brought a pillow and blanket from the closet. "It *is* morning," he said. We'd best turn off the T.V. and both of us hit the sack. Maybe we can catch an hour or two of sleep."

Elise yawned. "I must be getting old. I can't take these long hours anymore. Used to, I could go for days and not even mess up my makeup."

"Yeah, well, 'used to' didn't include the problems we've got with these long hours," Richard said as he started to ask ABBI to turn off the T.V.

"We interrupt this program for a special bulletin," the T.V. announcer suddenly intoned.

"What's this?"

Elise glanced casually at the large screen. The anchorwoman was standing in front of a news desk.

"Ladies and Gentlemen, we have just received word of an amazing story regarding the testing of the world's first time travel machine. There have been rumors for several days now, but our own Jan Stricker has some astounding information."

The lines around Elise's eyes tightened. Jan Stricker? Where had she heard that name?

"While all the details are unconfirmed at this time, it seems that the test of the time travel machine was not a complete failure as reported initially by officials at General Amalgamated Laboratories. And we have reports of a daring robbery at the labs. We go live to Jan outside General Amalgamated. Jan, what's going on?"

Elise staggered to the couch and sat down as Jan Stricker's face filled the screen. Chris woke up.

"The reporter at the lab!" Richard yelled.

"Thank you, Amber," Jan said. "My own investigative reporting led me to General Amalgamated Laboratories this evening, where I was able to uncover two amazing stories." She proceeded to tell the whole world of Chris' existence, and of something called a 'memory string' that was missing.

Elise was in shock. "What are we going to do? This place will be crawling with people any minute."

Richard shook his head. "We sure can't stay here... and I don't imagine my place would be any safer. We'll have to go to a motel. And I suggest we get out now."

Elise looked at Chris who was now wide awake. At the same instant they stood up and moved into action. Elise gathered up a change of clothes and her toothbrush and tossed them in an overnight bag. Chris got his uniform together while Elise emptied her gym bag to put it in. Although it only took minutes, Richard paced up and down waiting impatiently for them.

When everyone was ready, they hurried to the elevator and descended to the lobby. In their agitated state, all of them managed to miss a corpulent figure in the lobby, frantically trying to hide behind a large palm plant. They rushed out of the door.

Lou Ahn waited until they were outside before he roll-strolled over to the elevator. He could always pick them up later, but this might be his only chance to look over McAllister's apartment. He wasn't about to fall for that story of the memory string being 'lost'.

Once on the ninety-second floor, he went directly to Elise's door, fiddled with the lock but for a moment, and let himself in.

Twenty minutes later, with the apartment in shambles, he left, cursing to himself. He waited impatiently for the elevator, his pudgy finger punching the call button. When the elevator arrived and the doors opened, he was rudely pushed to the side by a throng of reporters, each struggling to be the first to talk to Doctor McAllister. Lou Ahn smiled as he rode down by himself.

Elise, Chris, and Richard drove around in circles for twenty minutes, trying to decide what to do. Chris was surprised at the number of cars on the streets even at this time of night.

Elise was all for heading straight for Professor Sanford's, but Richard argued that the press would be hounding him as well. Elise reluctantly agreed. The only logical solution seemed to be to get a motel room for the night. It was obvious that they couldn't just drive around for the next several hours.

They cruised the streets for another few minutes, looking for a suitable, nondescript motel. Elise finally spotted a motel that offered rooms by the night – week – month, with a V CANC sign lit up out front. She pulled in and parked next to an older model, red Chevrolet. Richard went to the office to secure a room for them.

A bell tinkled softly as Richard opened the office door, but no one appeared behind the counter.

"Hello? Anyone here?"

No answer. Richard called out again, louder. A door behind the counter opened and a sleepy-eyed, elderly man stared at Richard.

"What d'ya want?"

"A room, please."

"This time of night?"

Richard paused. "What is this? Twenty questions? Yes, this time of night, I want a room."

The clerk looked him over carefully. "Month?"

"No, I…"

"Week?"

Richard paused again. "No, I…"

"I thought so. Just you and a lady?"

Richard pursed his lips. "There's three of us."

The clerk shook his head. "No kids."

Richard was becoming impatient. "We have no kids."

The old man's eyes narrowed. "This is a class joint. We don't like funny stuff."

Richard took a step forward, his face tightly set.

"But it's none of my business what goes on between consenting adults," the clerk said quickly. He pushed a registration card toward Richard. "Fill this out."

Richard completed the card and accepted a key.

"Number twenty-three, upstairs."

Richard returned to the car, then led the way up to room number twenty-three. He almost tried the wrong door when he couldn't quite make out the broken number twenty-two, but finally, they tumbled into the right room.

They all fell asleep in their clothes, exhausted.

Chapter 14

It seemed like Professor Sanford had no more than put down his book and turned off his lamp, when the pounding on the door started. He clicked the light back on, sat up on the edge of his bed, and looked at the clock. Ten minutes after two. He put on his robe and hurried to the front door turning lights on as he went. The pounding knock hadn't ceased.

"Professor Milton Sanford?"

"You were expecting someone else?"

A man dressed in a dark suit and a woman, also in a dark suit, shouldered their way past him. They visually checked the room as they entered. "May we come in?"

"Who are you?"

The man pulled an identification wallet from his coat pocket. "Daniel Waring, C.I.A. This is Miranda Hartford, F.B.I."

The professor was more than a little puzzled. "F.B.I.? C.I.A.?"

Daniel Waring looked him right in the eye. "Professor, we have to speak to you in the strictest confidence about a matter concerning the security of the United States."

The professor waved the two government agents to chairs in the living room. "I'm afraid I don't understand. It's after two o'clock in the morning. What security?"

Waring took out a tablet and pen. "Professor, what can you

tell us about Doctor Elise McAllister?"

"Elise?"

Both agents nodded.

He closed his eyes. "Well, she's got dark brown hair, about so long…"

Hartford frowned. "We know her physical features, Professor. What we want to know is, what is she like? Her character."

The professor looked both agents over carefully. "I'm sorry. I must know what is going on. Is she in trouble? Has she done something wrong?"

There was a long pause before Waring spoke. "Professor, Doctor McAllister may have breached national security by stealing something called 'memory string plans' for the time travel vehicle she was developing."

Professor Sanford laughed. "Elise steal plans? Ridiculous! Besides, why not talk to her? And what does the time travel vehicle have to do with national security?"

"The U.S. Defense Cabinet, under the direction of the Secretary of Defense, has a lot of money tied up in that project. It's not unreasonable to assume that every foreign cartel in the world is also interested in the project. In fact, we have reason to believe that one of them has an agent, Double O-X, already working with someone within General Amalgamated Laboratories. Someone high up. We can't question Doctor McAllister because she and this memory string have disappeared. Two plus two, Professor, still add up to four. We know she and you are close friends. We know she visited you yesterday. We want to know what you talked about. What did she tell you?"

The professor sat back amazed.

Hartford leaned forward. "We know the phony story being circulated about a man from the past. We assume it is to attract attention away from the theft. Do you know where Doctor McAllister is, Professor?"

"But it's not a phony story! I talked to him myself."

Waring shook his head. "Don't feel bad, Professor. These are very clever people we're dealing with. What was the purpose of her visit?"

The Professor thought carefully. "She wanted to find two men."

"Two men? Who? Why?"

"There was some trouble..." He was torn between wanting to tell them the whole story to help Elise, and Elise's warning not to go to the police.

Waring ran a hand through his silver hair. "Professor Sanford, time is an urgent element here."

The Professor sat back tiredly in his chair. "She said not to contact the police... she had been warned..."

Waring cocked his head. "She had been warned? You mean Doctor McAllister? Warned by whom about what?" He could see the fear in the old man's eyes, but fear of what?... or from whom? "Professor, if someone is in danger, I think maybe you should give us the whole story."

The professor sighed and began his narrative... at least as much of it as he knew; the lost string, the kidnapping, Richard's arrest, help from Lou Ahn...

"Louann," Waring asked, "who is she?"

Professor Sanford smiled. "He is not a she. It's two names, Lou Ahn. He's a private investigator here in the city, and he's a friend of mine."

Hartford flipped back through her tablet. "Lou Ahn, that's the guy that did the initial on the break in at the lab. We'll check him out."

Waring and Hartford stood, and Waring shook hands with the professor.

"We appreciate your help in this matter, Professor. I would like to remind you, however, that some of what you have told us is classified material. Please don't repeat anything you heard here tonight. Do I make myself clear?"

The professor shook his head solemnly. "You'll let me know as soon as Elise turns up? I fear she may have been kidnapped now, too."

"We'll be in touch."

Lou Ahn popped a handful of peanuts into his mouth and leaned way back in his chair, going over the sequence of events. Somewhere, he must have overlooked something. A piece of the puzzle was missing. The memory string was also still missing. There was no way to tell how long he could stall off his superiors, and no telling how much longer Doctor Bruce was going to cooperate.

The original plan had been a masterpiece and nothing less. The implications of time travel; the ability to develop a weapon, then go back into time to deploy it before the enemy even knew of its existence, or to bring weapons of the future back to now... it was a staggering concept! However, the costs associated with developing a time travel vehicle were also staggering, not to mention the technology needed.

The obvious solution of letting the American government develop it and perfect it, then to steal it, was practically a foregone conclusion. Lou Ahn had no trouble 'persuading' Doctor Bruce to join the cause. It is amazing what the promise of very large sums of money will cause a man to do. It was under Doctor Bruce's directive that only one memory string was created that contained the massive set of plans for the vehicle... terabytes of data that would take several years for anyone to recreate ... the body of work that was on the single memory string that Doctor Bruce was to turn over upon a successful test of the vehicle. But blast the luck!... to put it in the mildest possible terms.

It all boiled down to either Elise McAllister had the string, or those clowns James and Gregory had it. McAllister had managed to slip out of sight, and that made her the prime candidate. But James and Gregory's whereabouts were known, so a little visit with them might not be out of order.

Lou Ahn yawned a great heaving yawn. It was late and he was tired. He hadn't even had time to watch the news on T.V.

tonight. Perhaps a few hours rest, then back on the trail. He decided to sleep on the specially made double cot in his office. Soon, he would be a very rich and powerful man.

Jan Stricker rubbed her eyes. A glance at the clock confirmed what she already knew. It was very late. She took another drink of coffee and grunted. It was cold.

All the wires and news services had picked up her story of the man from the past. The pressure was on for a follow-up. Trouble was, she could find no trace of this mysterious man, or Elise McAllister, for that matter. She hoped to God that she wasn't wrong about the whole thing. But she couldn't be. McAllister herself had said... only where was McAllister? Official confirmation (in the form of the actual man from the past) had to be made by McAllister, and now she had disappeared. Jan's face tightened. What if McAllister had been kidnapped? And what about the one part of the story Jan had kept to herself... Doctor Bruce's apparent involvement. If 'Double O-X' didn't sound sinister, she didn't know what did.

The mere thought of the intrigue sent shivers up her spine. Here at hand was the opportunity to be directly involved in one of the great mysteries of our time. A wild thought ran through her mind. She took out her pocket tel and looked up a number. Incredible. It was there! She dialed, waited, holding her breath, until a sleepy voice answered.

"Yes?"

Jan was suddenly very afraid. What was she going to say? She had to say something.

"Hello. Who's there?" The voice sounded impatient.

"Doctor Bruce?"

"Yes. What is it? Who is this?"

Jan almost hung up. Then a thought came into mind. Intrigue...

"I have a message from Double O-X." She held her breath.

There was a pause, then, "Is it cold out?"

A code! How could she possibly answer? What could the

reply be? Is it cold out?... of course not, 'it's summer', she wanted to say. So, she said it. She couldn't believe her ears when Doctor Bruce told her to go ahead. She must have given the right answer. How dumb were these crooks? But now what? She had no message.

"Has he got the string?" Doctor Bruce asked impatiently.

Jan plunged on. "Not yet. Doctor McAllister has disappeared."

There was a stream of curses that sizzled Jan's ears.

"That fat fool! You tell him to roll his giant body out of bed and find that string! I can't trace the cause of the malfunction without it, and until I make the corrections, it's no good to his people."

The tel went dead in Jan's hand as Doctor Bruce jammed the End Call button on his tel.

Jan slowly pushed her End Call, too. Fat fool? Giant body? His people? Something big was up, and it didn't take a detective to see what was going on. Doctor Bruce was a defector... or a spy... or something. And armed with that knowledge, Jan was prepared to... to... to what? What could she do?

First things first. She got up and poured herself a fresh cup of coffee, then sat down to rationalize. She began to make notes:

1. Doctor Bruce – defector?
2. Double O-X – foreign agent? (a fat man)
3. Missing memory string (?) – time machine plans?
4. Doctor McAllister - missing – why? – where?
5. A man from the past – really?
6. Now what?

McAllister had to be the key to this whole thing. Jan yawned. McAllister. She had to be found. Call it woman's intuition, but McAllister had all the answers. Jan was sure of that. But where is she?

She tried to put herself in McAllister's position. What

would I do if I wanted to hide? Go to a hotel? No. I'd probably go to some sleazy motel. No one would expect that of a respected scientist... no one but a certain journalist named Jan Stricker. There couldn't be more than a hundred sleazy motels in this city, and it was now, what time? She would start hunting at first light in the morning.

As she got ready for bed, she sleepily wondered about the man from the past. How did that part of the story manage to become secondary? What was memory string and why was it so important? Was espionage really more interesting than what this man represented? How was it that no one had caught even a glimpse of him? Could he be an elaborate fabrication to cover the theft and intrigue? So many questions, and so little time to sleep. She crawled into bed and quickly drifted off.

Chapter 15

A door slammed and Chris stirred.

Voices right outside the window brought him fully awake. He glanced around. Where was he? He sat up. Richard was soundly sleeping on the floor beside him. Elise was stretched out comfortably on the bed.

The voices passed their room. That's right, they were at an inn… or a motel, as Elise called it.

The sun was up, but a heavy curtain drawn closed across the window prevented any direct sunlight from filtering into the room. Chris stretched. One thing about modern clothes – they were uncomfortably tight. He stood and stretched again.

A car sputtered, then roared into life outside. He quietly stepped over Richard to the window and pulled the curtain aside. The red Chevrolet next to Elise's car was backing out. He watched it pull out of the parking lot with an eerie feeling that he somehow recognized the man on the passenger's side. He couldn't quite place the face, but he quit thinking about it when his stomach rumbled.

"All right you bunch of lazy mule drivers! Roll out!"

Richard rolled over enough that if he had been in bed, he probably would have fallen out.

Elise's eyelids fluttered.

"Up and attum, trooper!" Chris yelled.

Elise sat up and smiled. "Good morning."

Richard groaned. "A few more minutes, that's all…"

Chris jabbed at him with his foot. "Come on, trooper, out of the sack. I can see by the sun that we're a little runnin' late."

"Oh, no!" It was Elise. "A little late? Its twenty minutes to eight. We've got to get going."

Richard stood up. "What about breakfast?"

"There's no time. Chris, you've got to get changed into your uniform. It takes fifteen minutes just to drive to the warehouse."

Chris grabbed up his uniform and exited to the bathroom.

"Has anybody considered just how ludicrous this whole thing is?" Richard asked. "What are we going to do when we meet these characters?"

"We'll just have to play it by ear," Elise said.

Chris stepped out of the bathroom, buttoning up his shirt. "First of all, we are not going to meet these characters."

Richard stared at him. "We're not?"

"*We're* not. I am. And second, what I think Elise means, is right. I'll have to take it as it comes. These guys seem desperate, and that could work for us or against us."

"How so?" Elise asked.

Chris tied his on his red bandana, adjusted it to fit over his mouth and nose, then pushed it down around his neck. "If these desperados are anxious enough, maybe they'll take the goods and run. That's what I'm hoping for. On the other hand, they may want to examine the card to make sure they don't have to go through this much trouble again. That's what I'm hoping against."

Richard shook his head. "Don't you think we should have some sort of plan? I mean with just the basics, like what to do if they're armed, or they don't turn over Wende, or they find that the card is a fake? I don't want to rain on anybody's parade, but this could be a dangerous situation we're walking into with our eyes wide open. Captain, you're a military man. Don't you normally have a battle plan when you engage the enemy?"

The words struck home. Chris thought back to his last

moments with General Custer. They had been discussing battle plans… attack plans. And where was the General now? What good has his plans done him? No, in view of past events, it seemed most expedient to proceed on an 'as we go' footing. Besides, there was absolutely nothing to base a plan on.

Elise broke his thoughts. "We don't have any time to do any planning now, anyway. We've just got time to make it to the warehouse if we hurry."

Chris grabbed his hat and gun belt off the bed along with the bag containing his change of clothes.

Richard cautiously opened the front door and looked right, then left, then scanned the parking lot. No one was in sight. He blushed slightly as he realized that he felt a bit like a dashing commando on a raid. He led the way as the others followed him down to Elise's car.

They put Chris in the back seat, made him leave his hat off, and told him to slouch down. The less attention he attracted in his uniform, the better.

Richard insisted on driving. He backed the car from its space and pulled to the driveway. There was only one car coming, and it had its blinkers on to turn into the parking lot, so Richard pulled out.

Lou Ahn couldn't believe his eyes. As he pulled into the motel parking lot to see James and Gregory, Doctor McAllister's car pulled out. What incredible luck! Only what were they doing here? McAllister couldn't be in cahoots with those clowns, could she? Was there another cartel working behind the scenes? James and Gregory could wait. He couldn't lose McAllister again. His tires squealed and smoked as he spun a circle in the parking lot to follow their car.

Although he knew there was no way they could identify his car, they might recognize his bulk behind the wheel, so he stayed back several car lengths. From the way they were driving, hurriedly but straightforward, he knew they didn't suspect that they were being followed. Lou Ahn smiled. He wasn't down and out yet.

They all traveled straight down the street for several blocks, then Richard pulled in the left turn lane at the first main cross street. Lou Ahn let a car pull in between them, then pulled in behind.

Jan Stricker tapped her fingers on the steering wheel of her Martin 380Z as she waited impatiently for the light to change. Her search of motels was proving to be a fruitless, boring undertaking. She glanced in her rearview mirror, then ahead as the cars turning in front of her took off.

She did a classic double take as the first car made its turn. Sitting in the passenger's seat was none other than Doctor Elise McAllister! Jan couldn't believe it. Three cars made the turn. She was in the wrong lane for a right turn, but in no way was she going to let Doctor McAllister and associates get away.

Just as the light turned green, she stomped the gas pedal to the floor and shot into the intersection. Fortunately, the car to her right was not prone to jackrabbit starts, for Jan whipped her wheels around and cut across to follow McAllister's car. She pulled in behind some fat guy's car, three cars behind Elise's car. She had to smile at her luck. They drove for almost five minutes before being stopped by another light.

C.I.A. agent Daniel Waring pulled his agency car to the curb and turned to his partner. "It just doesn't make sense. With McAllister's face plastered all over the T.V. and newsfeeds, how does the woman just disappear?"

F.B.I. agent Miranda Hartford sat glumly in the passenger's seat unconsciously staring at every car that passed them.

Waring droned on. "We need to find her, or we need to have a little chat with that private eye... what was it?... oh, yeah, Lou Ahn. Somebody somewhere has to have some information on this crazy case. A time machine. Sheesh!"

The light in front of them turned green and the row of cars took off past them. Hartford's eyes narrowed, then flew wide open. She hit herself alongside of her head and let out a yelp.

Waring jumped. "What's the matter?"

"That car in the lead!"

Waring feigned excitement. "Yeah, and look, there's three cars behind it!"

"Mc...Mc... McAllister!" Hartford stammered.

"Are you sure?"

"I'm positive."

Waring gave a cursory look in the mirror and pulled out into the intersection just as his light turned red. He narrowly missed being broad-sided, shouted at no one in particular, and floor-boarded his poor old agency car. They shot off in pursuit of Doctor McAllister.

"There's no way she can make us, so get right behind her," Hartford managed to choke out, holding on for dear life.

Waring pulled in four cars back, waiting for an opening. It came soon when the car right behind Elise's car made a left turn.

Lou Ahn didn't want to get too close to McAllister, so he suddenly dropped back.

Jan had to react quickly to keep from rear-ending Lou Ahn. She stood on her brake pedal. Her car just bumped his.

C.I.A. agent Waring wasn't prepared. Without hitting his brakes at all, he smashed into Jan's car, throwing her car up onto the trunk of Lou Ahn's car.

Richard drove on, intent on getting where they needed to go, unaware of the chain reaction going on behind them.

Lou Ahn had the breath mostly knocked out of him when he was thrown violently against the steering wheel. He sat slumped over, gasping for air.

Jan's neck felt as if someone had jabbed a thousand needles into it. Her head had snapped forward, then back sharply, when Waring's car crunched into hers. It wasn't a major case of whiplash, but it was enough that she'd have a major headache for the rest of today and part of tomorrow.

Agent Waring bruised his forehead and opened a small gash above his right eye during his brief contact with the windshield.

Only F.B.I. agent Hartford wasn't hurt. She had slid off the seat onto the floor. She made sure that Waring wasn't hurt badly, then scrambled out of the car and ran up to Jan's car. Waring followed groggily.

Hartford pulled open the door. "Miss, are you all right?" She looked at Jan anxiously.

Jan opened her eyes, focused on Hartford, and asked, "Why did you hit me? Didn't you see my brake lights?"

"I didn't hit you," Hartford assured her. "How do you feel?"

"I think my neck is broken."

"Stay where you are." Hartford ran up to Lou Ahn's car. "Hey, buddy, are you all right?"

The immense figure behind the wheel was still gasping for air but was definitely getting his breath back. "I must follow that car," he muttered.

Hartford looked down the street. McAllister's car was nowhere to be seen.

Lou Ahn struggled to sit up right. He reached in his coat pocket and pulled out a business card. He mustn't let McAllister get away. "Here," he said to the stranger, "this is my card. You'll have to contact me later. I'm on official business."

Hartford took the card. Her eyes widened. "Hey! You're the guy..." She never finished her sentence.

Lou Ahn put his car into gear and slowly pulled away with a terrible screeching and tearing of metal. He pulled out from under Jan's car, and lumbered on down the street, Hartford yelling after him.

Waring had to dance to the side so Jan's car didn't drop on him. He ran up to Hartford. "He can't do that! That's hit and run!"

"That's the guy!" Hartford shouted.

"What guy?"

"Lou Ahn, the private eye!"

Waring didn't hesitate. He ran back to his agency car and jumped in. The engine started right up. He jammed it into reverse and gave it the gas, pulling away from Jan's car, but only after ripping her back bumper off. It dangled from his own front bumper.

Jan jumped out of her car. "What are you doing?" she screamed.

Hartford ran past her. She thrust Lou Ahn's card into her hand. "Everything's all right. Just call this man. His insurance will handle everything." She got in the agency car, and Waring sped off, Jan's bumper banging on the pavement.

Jan stomped her feet in frustration. "Why is there never a cop around when you want one?" she screamed.

No other cars had even come by. There was little traffic out here in the industrial section of the city, even at this time of the morning.

Jan got back in her car, but the engine wouldn't turn over. They usually don't when the fan gets jammed up into the radiator. She rubbed her neck and finally looked at the card in her hand. 'Lou Ahn – Private Detective.'

She almost fainted. Lou Ahn! Doctor McAllister! She fumbled for her purse and her pocket tel. Once found, she dialed frantically. "Bendt? Shut up and listen. I need a car and a camera unit quick!"

Richard followed Elise's directions to the warehouse. There was an older model, red Chevrolet already parked out front. Chris thought there was something vaguely familiar about the car, but other thoughts pushed it from his mind. Richard pulled in behind it and shut off the engine. They all stared at the warehouse.

No one moved until Elise prodded them. "We're supposed to be inside right now."

Chris opened his door. "*I'm* supposed to be inside. You two stay here."

Elise opened her door and got out. "You're going in alone?"

Chris nodded.

"Over my dead body." She turned and started walking towards the building.

Richard got out to join Elise.

Chris quickly strapped on his gun and sword belt, and put on his wide brimmed, floppy hat. He checked his pocket for the phony memory card, then ran to catch up with the others.

They stood at the back door and stared up at the broken window.

"We have to go in that way?" Richard asked hesitantly.

"You got it," Chris told him. "I'd just as soon not go dancing in the front door. There's nothin' to it. We just roll this barrel over here, jump up on it, and climb through." He pulled the metal drum back under the window. "I'll go first."

Since the metal was still cool in the morning air, and the glass was all removed from the window and sill, Chris hopped nimbly through the opening. The office was deserted. He took note that it was quiet in here. The climate control contraption must be off. He whispered for Richard to come next. Richard stood on the barrel and was halfway through the window when Elise asked, "How did they get in?"

Chris hadn't thought about that. And now that he thought of it, the barrel wasn't where he had left it. He couldn't hide his surprise when the door opened, and Elise stepped into the office. Apparently, James and Greg had picked the lock and just left it open. Chris grinned sheepishly and helped Richard down. No one spoke.

Chris had wanted to survey the area first, if possible, before James and Greg knew they had arrived. He signaled for Elise and Richard to wait while he did his scouting.

The lights were still off in the building, so Chris had to let his eyes adjust to the darkness before he could follow the footprints in the dust on the floor. There were three sets of prints besides his own from yesterday (yesterday? Whew! Things surely did move fast in this world). So, the others were already here.

He was almost halfway down the wide center aisle when he saw them. In the dim light he couldn't make out their features clearly, but all three of them were there, standing. One of them was gesturing and must have been speaking, but Chris couldn't make out what they were saying. He eased himself back to the office.

"Did you see them?" Elise asked as soon as Chris shut the office door. "Did you see Wende?"

Chris nodded. "They're about three quarters down the center aisle." He pulled his gun out of its holster and handed it to Richard.

Richard stared at it.

"Take it," Chris urged. "I've got my sword, although I'm not really expecting them to give me any trouble."

"If you're not expecting any trouble, then why do I need this?"

"If what I expected always happened, I wouldn't be here discussing this right now. I'd be in the Montana Territory." He looked at Elise. "That is, if there is still a Montana Territory."

Elise shook her head. "It's a state."

Chris shook his head. "A state. Well, I guess I…"

Richard grabbed the pistol. "Couldn't we discuss this another time?"

"Yeah. I reckon they're liable to be gettin' a little restless. Now, listen close. Like I figured, they're staying away from the windows and the light. That's gonna to work to our advantage."

"It is?"

"You two go down a side aisle and stay out of sight until I need you… *if* I need you." He opened the office door and stepped back into the main warehouse. Elise and Richard followed. When their eyes adjusted to the darkness, they started down a side aisle. Every step they took made a little 'poof' in the dust on the floor.

None of them were aware that Lou Ahn had finally found their car and was at that very moment hurrying around the building and having seen the barrel in front of the window, was looking for an open door.

Chris walked slowly down the center aisle until he could just make out the figures of James, Gregory, and Wende. He stopped, then called out, "Hello the camp!"

Gregory was startled. James checked his watch in the dim light. "He's almost ten minutes late. You two get back out of sight. And we'll have no funny business out of you, young lady. Gregory will be with you at all times."

Gregory pulled Wende back into the shadows, behind a large stack of pipe.

James pulled his blond wig into place, straightened his blue simulated civil war uniform (which as close as he could come due to a production being put on by a local theater group. Most all western costumes were in use), and called out to Chris, "Right down here, Captain! Center aisle."

Chris waited a moment then walked up to James. He almost laughed but checked himself. Even in the dim light, he could see that James was dressed in an ungainly looking blue uniform, gold braids hanging from both shoulders and across his chest. His blond wig was fixed up into tight curls. It was the most ridiculous thing Chris had ever seen. He saluted the absurd figure.

James pulled himself up straight and casually returned the salute. "Captain, I'm pleased to see you." His voice cracked as he tried to mimic a gravelly voice of authority.

Chris fought back a grin. "My pleasure, sir. How are Major Reno and Captain Benteen, if I may ask?"

A brief look of panic crossed James' face, then he remembered. According to the web site, they had been Chris' fellow officers. James cleared his throat. "They're just fine, Captain, but that's not what I came here to talk to you about. We have important business to discuss." James wanted to get away from any historical discussion before he slipped up and trapped himself. "Captain, we've been together for a long time, haven't we?" It was a question, but he quickly turned it into a statement. "I mean, haven't we."

Over a hundred and fifty years, Chris thought. "Yes sir, we have."

"I may never have said this before, but I've always considered you one of my favorite officers."

Chris choked but turned it into a polite cough.

"Captain, I'd like to ask you a favor, man to man."

Chris pulled the phony memory card from his pocket. "I believe this is what you want, sir?"

James stared at the small card. It was the right size. Yes, that had to be it! "Excellent, my boy, excellent." James dropped his gruff voice in his excitement. "Where did you find it?"

Chris caught a movement behind James. That would be Greg and Wende. "Well, sir, it's a long story." He pulled the card back from James' outstretched hand and glanced casually to his right. There was a flicker of movement. Elise and Richard. Chris hoped they would stay where they were, out of sight. He was aware also of a click as the climate control unit cycled on and the overhanging canvas tubes began to swell with air moving through them.

James was growing visibly impatient. "Well, it doesn't really matter. The important thing is that you have it and you're going to give it to me." He reached out again.

"Sir, I asked you to look into the disappearance of a friend of mine, Miss Merrill. Did you get a chance to do that?" Chris held the card tantalizingly out of reach.

James couldn't stand the torture. "Yes, she's yours as soon as you give me that card!"

"She's here?"

James' eyes never left the card. "Miss Merrill!"

Wende stepped forward. "Captain…"

"I'll take the card, Captain. That's an order!"

Chris smiled at Wende and started to give the card to James.

"I'll take that!" a voice in the darkness boomed.

James and Chris both whirled towards the voice.

"Who said that?" James demanded.

Lou Ahn stepped into the dim light. "Double O-X… and I'll take that, now if you please." He held a shiny Smith and Wesson .38. "Congratulations, Captain, on tracing down the elusive set of plans. You have succeeded where even I have failed, until now. Where's the string?"

"What this about string?" James asked puzzled.

"Don't be so sure of that, Double Ox." Gregory stepped up holding a small caliber pistol, pointing it directly at Lou Ahn.

"That's Double O-X!" Lou Ahn snorted.

James smiled. "Well, now, we seem to be in a bit of a stalemate, don't we?"

Chris heard a movement behind him and smiled.

"Not exactly," a voice said.

Chris frowned. That wasn't Richard's voice.

C.I.A. agent Daniel Waring stepped into the light. "Please lower your weapons, gentlemen."

They did.

"Now, I think there are a few little things I'd like to have cleared up," Waring said.

"Maybe you could start by dropping your gun and telling us who you are and how you're involved in this," Richard said as he joined the group, brandishing Chris' .45.

"Maybe he doesn't need to," F.B.I. agent Miranda Hartford said from her hiding place. "Why don't you drop yours instead."

"This has gone far enough!" James shouted. He grabbed Wende and held a penknife to her throat. "Everybody, drop your weapons!" he commanded. "This is a circus, for crying out loud. Drop them!"

There were five distinct thuds as the guns struck the dust covered cement floor.

Gregory spoke as he reached for his .22. He had dropped it when James' voice boomed out the command. It was instinct. "Good move, James. I didn't even know that you carried a knife."

"Shut up, you fool," James snapped, "and leave that gun where it is."

Gregory stopped, stooped over, and twisted his head around to look at James. "What are you talkin' about?"

"I said, leave the gun."

"James, this is me, Gregory, your partner. Maybe you can't

see me so good in the bad light."

"I can see you just fine. Stand up."

There was a coldness in the voice that Gregory had never heard before. He straightened up, surprised. "What's goin' on? You're actin' crazy."

James sneered. "Crazy like a fox. Captain, I'll take that card now." His eyes were hard.

Chris faced him, staring him down.

A bead of sweat broke out on James' forehead even though the climate control was system was operating. "Captain, let's be reasonable, shall we? That card is no good to you. Neither is Miss Merrill if you don't comply. As your commanding officer, I order you to hand over that card!"

"We're partners," Gregory whined. "Let me take it from him."

James whirled on him. "Shut up, you blubbering fool. I don't need any help from..." He jumped at a flashing movement and the sound of metal against metal.

Chris held his sword with the point an inch in front of James' face. The metal gleamed in the dim light. No one moved. No one spoke. Everyone stared at the point of the sword. It was unwavering in James' face, and a glint of light flashed on something stuck to and hanging from the very point.

Wende gasped and reached out. "The memory string," she said breathlessly. "It was in the scabbard." She plucked it off the sword and held it up.

James snapped out of his shocked state and looked at Chris. "But you had..."

"A fake," someone said.

James reached for the string. "So, what is this?"

Wende immediately stuck the string down the front of her blouse. James let go of her throat and twirled her around, facing him. When he let go of her, there was a mad scramble as everyone dropped to the floor to grab their weapons. They all came up at the same time. No one knew who to point their weapon at for sure, so everyone waved and pointed guns at one another as they shouted commands to disarm. It was quickly obvious no one was going to relinquish their weapon.

"I hope you're happy," James sneered at everyone. "Now we're back to stalemate."

Wende took a step closer to Chris.

Several voices told her to stop right where she was.

James closed his eyes and rubbed the bridge of his nose. "Ladies and gentlemen, I'm sure that we can come to some sort of understanding as to who is going to get those plans. Now, I think it's obvious that I want it very badly. I've gone to great lengths ..."

"Then it *was* you," Lou Ahn said. "You bungled the job at the laboratory."

James was surprised. "How do you... you! You were the one who interrupted us."

"But I thought you were the one investigating the whole thing," Richard said. "You arrested me when you knew all along that I had nothing to do with the disappearance of the memory card."

Both Daniel Waring and Miranda Hartford trained their guns on Lou Ahn. Waring spoke. "Well, Mr. Lou Ahn, also known as agent Double O-X, we've been looking for you for a long time."

"Who are you?" James asked.

Waring pulled out his identification, even though it was much too dark to read it. "Daniel Waring, C.I.A. This is my partner, Miranda Hartford, F.B.I."

Wende's jaw dropped. "C.I.A.? F.B.I.?"

"We'll take that string, Mr. ... whoever you are."

"Why do *you* want the string?" Richard asked.

"It will be turned over to the Secretary of Defense."

"The Secretary of Defense?"

"That time machine is of priceless value for military uses."

Elise's knees almost buckled. She had stayed out of sight hiding. Military uses? No one had said anything about the military being involved. It had great historical uses, but the military? She wondered if Doctor Bruce was aware of this.

"You don't really think Doctor Bruce is going to just sit back and let this string be handed around, do you?" Wende asked. "After all, this project was his idea."

"Not quite."

Wende frowned at Lou Ahn. "What do you mean?"

Lou Ahn smiled smugly. "Your good Doctor Bruce was working under orders from the same cartel that I work for. None of this would be taking place if he had gotten the string to me before you messed up everything."

Elise, Richard, and Wende were stunned.

"You mean Doctor Bruce is a spy?" Wende murmured.

"We've suspected as much for some time," said Waring. "It was only a matter of time before we broke the whole thing open."

Elise couldn't believe it. Tears sprang to her eyes. How could she have been involved for so long and not suspected anything? She leaned against the pile of dirty pipe for support. One of the end pipes slipped a little. She stared at it, then grabbed it with both hands. It was definitely loose. Ideas began rushing into her head. She grabbed the pipe again and pulled as hard as she could.

As soon as Chris heard the scrape of pipe behind him, he guessed what was about to happen. He grabbed Wende and threw her towards Richard. There were several shouts, but they were drowned out by the crashing, smashing of an entire pallet of clay pipe collapsing. Dust filled the air.

Richard took Wende and dodged behind a pile of pipe.

Another pile collapsed.

A shot rang out.

Everyone was coughing from the clouds of fine dust erupted by the collapsing piles of pipe. Chris pulled his bandana over his nose and mouth and, with a couple of steps, jumped to the top of a pile of pipe. He was within reach of the canvas air duct for the climate control system. With one hefty swing of his sword, he cut the canvas in two. The duct fell, blowing air in two directions, further stirring up clouds of dust.

No one could see, no one could breathe. Shouts broke off into coughing fits.

Chris adjusted his bandana. He had never seen so much dust, even when riding through thick prairie dust storms. He felt his way down off the stack of pipe. There were two people on the floor in front of him. It was Richard and Wende. He grabbed Richard's arm and pulled him to his feet. He only hoped that Richard still had hold of Wende. Chris couldn't see any better than anyone else, but because of his bandana, at least he could breathe. The dust blotted out what light there was. He stumbled in the darkness, towing Richard and Wende behind him. At least he hoped it was them.

Years of riding alone on the plains had developed Chris' sense of direction to an uncanny fineness. He headed for where he figured Elise ought to be. She was there, behind the piles of collapsed pipe, gasping for breath. Chris took her hand, too, and led all three of them towards the back of the building, the office, and the door.

Chris was aware of a rumbling noise, and suddenly, the dust behind them seemed to light up. An explosion and fire? There were shouts from the other end of the building. He lost Elise's hand, then Richard's. He was on his own.

Jan Stricker, her cameraman, and several cops stood in front of the massive open overhead door. A cloud of dust immediately covered them, reducing them to coughing bodies, stumbling back. They looked in wonder at the clouds of dust billowing from the building's interior.

James and Gregory stumbled out first. Jan squealed in delight when she saw James in his uniform. She directed her cameraman to get his every movement. At last, proof of the man from the past.

Lou Ahn and Daniel Waring came out next. Lou Ahn followed and dropped to the ground, desperately gasping for air. The cops disarmed each man as they stumbled out.

Hartford came out next, wracked with coughing.

Elise thought she was dying. The dust burned her nose and throat. Someone took her arm and pulled her to her feet. She followed along behind them blindly. Then the grip was gone. She fell again. Two more bodies stumbled into her. She recognized Wende crying and tried to call out. All she could do was cough. She blindly grabbed Wende's hand, found it, and started crawling towards the new light at the end of the building. Finally, she broke into fresh air. Hands pulled her away from the building. Her lungs burned as she gulped in great lungs of fresh air. Wende and Richard lay beside her.

Jan was in her glory. All of the coughing men were spewing out stories of the missing memory string, in-between their coughing fits. Both stories were being filmed to a spectacular finish. She couldn't keep her eyes off James. She had expected a man from the past to be a little more rugged looking. This guy was pale and... well, wimpy.

The police handcuffed everyone who had been armed. They were amazed at the small arsenal and kept asking questions about what was going on.

Confusion reigned.

Jan got her cameraman set and started her story. "Good morning. This is Jan Stricker for W.R.A.P. with a big wrap-up for those of you who have been following my story of a spectacular robbery of a computer memory string from General Amalgamated Laboratories just two days ago. General Amalgamated has also been in the news with rumors of a man brought from the past with their new Time Travel Vehicle. Right here, today, I have not only the answer to the missing string, but live, with me, the mysterious man from the past!"

The cameraman swung around to James who sat, scowling.

Elise rolled over to Wende and whispered, "Do you still have the memory string?"

Wende, who had her breath now, nodded slightly and took it from her blouse. She handed it to Elise.

Richard sat up. "Where's Chris?"

Elise, in her excitement, hadn't missed him. Now her heart

skipped a beat. He must still be inside! She struggled to her feet. A policeman immediately stepped to her side grabbing her arm.

"Just a minute, ma'am," he said in a no-nonsense tone, "nobody goes anyplace until we get this whole thing straightened out."

Elise stared at the open door.

Another policeman joined them. "Which one of you is Miss Merrill?"

Wende got to her feet. "I am."

The cop looked almost apologetic. "It seems to be the general consensus that you have the stolen memory string."

Everyone gathered around her. Someone said, "It's in her blouse."

Wende looked embarrassed for a moment, then reached inside her blouse. A look of alarm crossed her face.

"Something the matter?" the cop asked.

"I seem to have lost it," Wende stuttered. "It must have fallen out inside the building!"

There were loud groans from all around.

Elise smiled inwardly and winked at Wende.

Jan was the most disappointed. She took up her story again. "The case of the missing computer memory string may have had a disastrous finish, but..." she brightened, "we still have our interview with the man from the past." She edged over to James. "Can you tell us, sir, who are you and where are you from?"

James sneered into the camera. "I'm James Bench, and I'm from the Royal Palms Motel at 1172 Freeport Drive."

Jan blinked. "What?" Her voice was strangely calm.

"I'm not from the past, you idiot! Ask him!" He pointed to Gregory.

Gregory sniffed. "I never saw him before in my life."

Jan sputtered into the camera. "But... then it was a... hoax? You're not from the past? ... My Pulitzer prize!"

Elise was worried about Chris. If he was still inside the building... she took advantage of the police officer's distraction to work her way to the edge of the building. She peered inside. Dust still boiled up. She stood back, fighting back tears. Then she heard a shout. Someone was standing near her car, waving his arms.

Elise did a double take. It was Chris... and he had changed clothes. She ran to him. They fell into each other's arms and kissed.

"I thought you were still inside," Elise said at last.

Chris chuckled. "When I lost you, I figured I'd best go get some help. Only when I got outside, help was already here. They had the whole other end of the building opened up, so I just slipped over here and changed clothes in your car."

Elise laughed with relief.

"What happened to the memory string?" Chris asked.

Elise pulled it out of her pocket. "Everyone thinks it was lost inside the building."

"What happens now?"

Elise handed it to him. "Whatever you think. Its loss would set us back years."

Chris took it and stared at it. His only hope for returning home lay in his hand. He looked around to a grate in the pavement. He stood over the storm drain, looked at the tiny piece of string, looked at Elise, and let it slip between his fingers and through the holes in the grate.

He smiled. "Now what?"

Elise smiled and took his hand.

ABOUT THE AUTHOR

John Meyers is retired except for his career as an author. He lives in Trinidad, Ca. with his wife, Sheryl. She also writes. Sometimes, they write together. Look them up at www.mosscanyon.com.

Made in the USA
Columbia, SC
23 September 2024

42869196R00108